SPECTRUM®

Critical Thinking for Math

Grade 1

Published by Spectrum®
an imprint of Carson Dellosa Education
Greensboro, NC

Spectrum®
An imprint of Carson Dellosa Education
P.O. Box 35665
Greensboro, NC 27425 USA

ISBN 978-1-4838-3548-8

02-286207784

Table of Contents Grade 1

Check What You Know

Addition and Subtraction Through 10

Add or subtract. Draw a picture to show your thinking.

1. 5
    + 1

2. 8
    − 6

Add or subtract. Use a number line to show your thinking.

3. 9
    − 4

4. 2
    + 3

5. Write the number sentences for each fact family given.

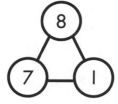

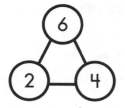

_____

_____

_____

_____

Check What You Know

Addition and Subtraction Through 10

Solve the problem below and show your work.

6. Jenny has 6 pennies. Her brother gives her 2 more pennies. When Jenny goes to the store, she wants to buy a juice box that costs 7 cents. Will Jenny be able to buy the juice box? Explain how you know. Draw a picture to help you solve.

Solve to find out how much more money is needed. Draw a picture to show your thinking.

7. ⬤ + _____ = 4 cents

8. ⬤⬤⬤⬤ ⬤⬤⬤ + _____ = 9 cents

Solve. Write the addition problem used and draw a picture to help you.

9.   7 – 2 = _____   _____ + _____ = _____

Lesson 1.1 Using Pictures to Add

To add 4 + 2, start by drawing four objects. Then, draw two more objects. Count the objects you have drawn altogether. The number you count is the total.

$$4 + 2 = 6$$

Add. Draw a picture to show your thinking.

2 + 1 =

2 + 2 =

1 + 5 =

3 + 0 =

Lesson 1.2   Using Pictures to Subtract

To subtract 5 – 2, start by drawing five objects. Then, cross out the number of objects you are subtracting. Count the objects you have not crossed out. The number you have left is the difference.

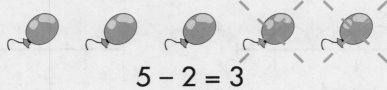

$$5 - 2 = 3$$

Subtract. Draw a picture to show your thinking.

2 – 1 =

4 – 3 =

5 – 2 =

3 – 1 =

Lesson 1.3   Using a Number Line to Add and Subtract

You can use a number line to add and subtract.

2 + 4 = ?

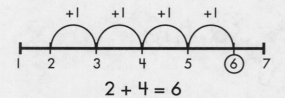

2 + 4 = 6

5 – 1 = ?

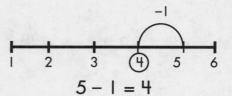

5 – 1 = 4

Add or subtract. Use a number line to show your thinking.

1 + 3 =

2 + 2 =

3 – 2 =

1 – 0 =

Lesson 1.4   Fact Families

A fact family is a collection of related addition or subtraction facts made from the same numbers.

You can use objects or drawings to help solve the problems.

$$\begin{array}{r} 2 \\ + 3 \\ \hline 5 \end{array} \qquad \begin{array}{r} 3 \\ + 2 \\ \hline 5 \end{array} \qquad \begin{array}{r} 5 \\ - 2 \\ \hline 3 \end{array} \qquad \begin{array}{r} 5 \\ - 3 \\ \hline 2 \end{array}$$

Add or subtract. Draw a picture to show your thinking.

$$\begin{array}{r} 3 \\ + 1 \\ \hline \end{array} \qquad \begin{array}{r} 1 \\ + 3 \\ \hline \end{array} \qquad \begin{array}{r} 4 \\ - 3 \\ \hline \end{array} \qquad \begin{array}{r} 4 \\ - 1 \\ \hline \end{array} \qquad\qquad \begin{array}{r} 1 \\ + 2 \\ \hline \end{array} \qquad \begin{array}{r} 2 \\ + 1 \\ \hline \end{array} \qquad \begin{array}{r} 3 \\ - 1 \\ \hline \end{array} \qquad \begin{array}{r} 3 \\ - 2 \\ \hline \end{array}$$

$$\begin{array}{r} 4 \\ + 1 \\ \hline \end{array} \qquad \begin{array}{r} 1 \\ + 4 \\ \hline \end{array} \qquad \begin{array}{r} 5 \\ - 4 \\ \hline \end{array} \qquad \begin{array}{r} 5 \\ - 1 \\ \hline \end{array} \qquad\qquad \begin{array}{r} 5 \\ + 1 \\ \hline \end{array} \qquad \begin{array}{r} 1 \\ + 5 \\ \hline \end{array} \qquad \begin{array}{r} 6 \\ - 5 \\ \hline \end{array} \qquad \begin{array}{r} 6 \\ - 1 \\ \hline \end{array}$$

Lesson 1.4 Fact Families

You can create your own fact family. Choose two numbers to add together. Then, you can write four number sentences that are true for that fact family.

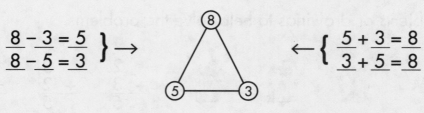

$$\left.\begin{array}{l} \underline{8} - \underline{3} = \underline{5} \\ \underline{8} - \underline{5} = \underline{3} \end{array}\right\} \rightarrow \qquad \leftarrow \left\{\begin{array}{l} \underline{5} + \underline{3} = \underline{8} \\ \underline{3} + \underline{5} = \underline{8} \end{array}\right.$$

Create your own fact family triangles. Write the addition and subtraction sentences that go with each family.

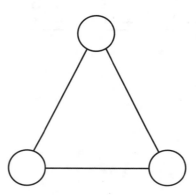

_____

_____

_____

_____

_____

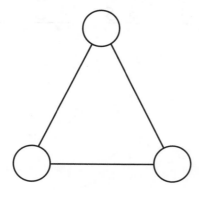

_____

_____

_____

_____

_____

Lesson 1.5 Addition in the Real World

When reading a problem, look for these keywords that tell you to add.

Addition Keywords
add   altogether   both   more   all   total   sum

Solve the problems and show your work. Circle the keywords in the problem that tell you to add.

Fuji has 4 dolls. Ana has 3 dolls. They can only fit 6 dolls in their doll carriage. Will all the dolls fit?

Betsy has 6 pink flowers. Drew has 1 pink flower. If Drew picks 1 more flower, will they have enough to make a bouquet with a total of 10 pink flowers?

Lesson 1.6 Subtraction in the Real World

When reading a problem, look for these keywords that tell you to subtract.

Subtraction Keywords
difference   fewer   how many/much more   left   less   minus   remains   away

Solve the problems and show your work. Circle the keywords in the problem that tell you to subtract.

There are 8 cars in the parking lot. 2 cars drive away. Then, 5 more drive away. How many cars are left in the parking lot?

Tia and Dante bought 10 apples to make an apple cobbler. Tia peeled 5 of the apples. Dante peeled 2. How many apples are left to peel?

Lesson 1.7   Adding with Coins

I penny

1¢

I nickel

5¢

I dime

10¢

5 pennies
5 cents

Add the amounts together and write how much money. Draw the coins to show your thinking.

2 pennies, I nickel

_____ cents

2 nickels

_____ cents

I nickel, 3 pennies

_____ cents

Lesson 1.7 Adding with Coins

How much more money is needed to reach the total?

4 pennies = 4 cents. Count on from 4 to determine how much more money is needed.

 + ? = 8 cents

? = 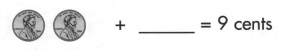 . Four more pennies are needed to make 8 cents.

Solve to find out how much more money is needed. Draw a picture to show your thinking.

 + _____ = 9 cents

 + _____ = 6 cents

Lesson 1.8 Coins in the Real World

John has 3 pennies. Ana has 2 pennies. How much money do they have altogether?

Drawing a picture can help you solve the problem.

John and Ana have 5 pennies altogether.

Solve the problems. Show your work.

Victor has 2 pennies. Then, he finds 6 more pennies. Can he buy a piece of candy that costs 7 cents? Explain how you know.

Lin has 5 pennies. Barb has 6 cents. Lin says she has the same amount of money as Barb, but Barb disagrees. Who is correct? Explain how you know.

Lesson 1.9 Using Addition for Subtraction

To solve the problem 8 − 4, turn it into an addition problem: 4 + ? = 8.

Draw 4 objects. Then, draw and count on more objects until you reach the total of 8.

Solve. Write the addition problem used and draw a picture to help you.

10 − 3 = _____   _____ + _____ = _____

8 − 2 = _____   _____ + _____ = _____

7 − 2 = _____   _____ + _____ = _____

Lesson 1.9   Using Addition for Subtraction

To solve the problem $9 - 7$, turn it into an addition problem: $7 + ? = 9$.

Draw 7 tally marks. Then, draw and count on more tallies until you reach the total of 9.

$\cancel{||||} || + ||$

It took 2 more tally marks to make 9. So, $7 + 2 = 9$, and $9 - 7 = 2$.

Solve. Write the addition problem used and draw tally marks to help you.

$5 - 1 =$ _____   _____ + _____ = _____

$10 - 4 =$ _____   _____ + _____ = _____

$8 - 5 =$ _____   _____ + _____ = _____

Check What You Learned

Addition and Subtraction Through 10

Add or subtract. Draw a picture to show your thinking.

1.
$$\begin{array}{r} 8 \\ -\ 4 \\ \hline \end{array}$$

2.
$$\begin{array}{r} 3 \\ +\ 4 \\ \hline \end{array}$$

Add or subtract. Use a number line to show your thinking.

3.
$$\begin{array}{r} 8 \\ +\ 1 \\ \hline \end{array}$$

4.
$$\begin{array}{r} 9 \\ -\ 6 \\ \hline \end{array}$$

5. Jasmine has 3 pennies. Marcus has 1 nickel. How much money do they have altogether? Draw a picture to help you solve.

Check What You Learned

Addition and Subtraction Through 10

Solve the problem and show your work.

6. Jan had 4 dolls sitting on a shelf. The dog ran off with 2 of the dolls. Jan was able to find 1 of the dolls outside in the doghouse. How many dolls does Jan have now?

Solve. Write the addition problem used and draw a picture to help you. Then, fill out the fact family triangle. Use the triangle to write one more addition problem and one more subtraction problem.

7. $7 - 5 =$ _____   _____ + _____ = _____

_____ − _____ = _____   _____ + _____ = _____

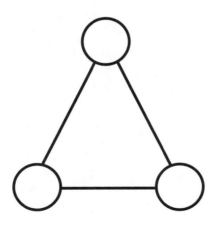

NAME _____

Check What You Know

Counting and Place Value

Draw each number with ones and tens blocks.

1. 76

2. 31

3. Count forward or backward. Write the missing numbers. Explain how you knew to count forward or backward.

113, _____, 111, _____, _____, _____, 107, 106, _____, 104

Break each number down into tens and ones. Determine which number is larger. Write **<**, **>**, or **=** in the box.

4. 46 ☐ 75

Lesson 2.1   Counting and Writing Numbers

Color 5 of the fish green.

Write the number you colored on the line.   __5__

Color the number given. Then, write the number colored on the line.

32

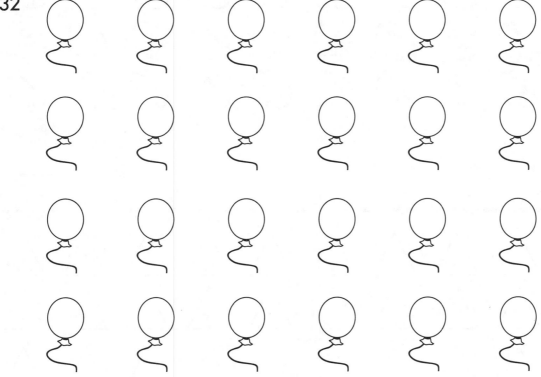

_____

Lesson 2.1   Counting and Writing Numbers

Color the number given. Then, write the number colored on the line.

55

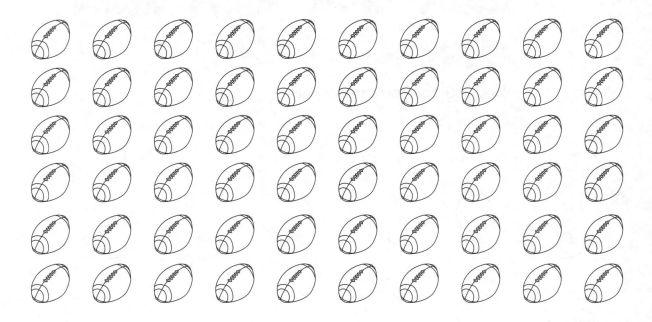

_____

27

_____

Lesson 2.2   Counting with Ones and Tens

You can use ones and tens blocks to show numbers.

■ = 1

1 one

= 10

1 ten

= 23

2 tens, 3 ones

Draw each number with ones and tens blocks.

27

58

Lesson 2.2 Counting with Ones and Tens

Draw each number with ones and tens blocks.

77

93

39

50

21

46

Lesson 2.3 Counting Forward

To count forward from 15, count on 1 apple to get 16. Keep counting on 1 for each apple.

| 15 | **16** | **17** | **18** | **19** | **20** | **21** | **22** | **23** | **24** | **25** | **26** |

Count forward from 78. Label each peach with a number.

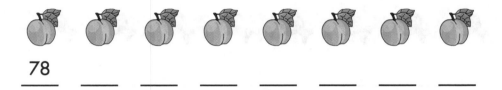

78 ___ ___ ___ ___ ___ ___ ___

Follow the path to count forward. Write the correct number in each circle.

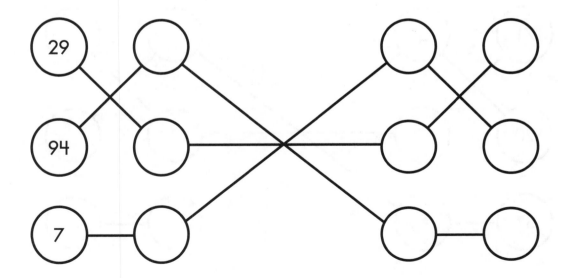

Lesson 2.4 Counting Backward

To count backward from 29, take away 1 to get 28. Keep taking away 1 for each cat.

29   **28**   **27**   **26**   **25**

Count backward from 46. Label each fish with a number.

46 ___ ___ ___ ___ ___ ___ ___ ___ ___

Follow the path to count backward. Write the correct number in each circle.

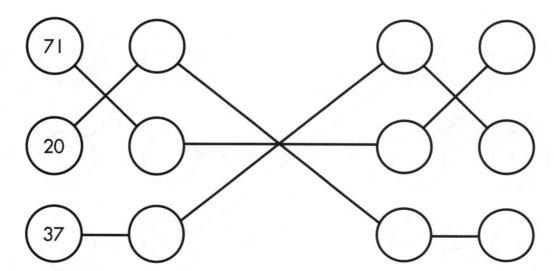

Lesson 2.5   Counting Forward and Backward

Count forward or backward. Write the missing number. Explain how you knew to count forward or backward.

46, 47, _____, 49, _____, _____, 52, 53, 54, _____, _____

102, 103, _____, _____, 106, 107, _____, _____, _____, 111, _____

59, _____, 57, 56, _____, 54, _____, _____, 51, 50, _____

99, _____, _____, _____, 95, 94, _____, _____, _____, 90

Lesson 2.6 Counting to 120

Count forward. Write the missing numbers.

1			4	5			8		10
	12		14		16			19	20
21		23							
31						37	38		
	42				46				50
		53			56			59	
				65	66			69	70
71								79	
		83				87	88		
91									100
	102					107			
			114						120

Spectrum Critical Thinking for Math
Grade 1

Lesson 2.6
Counting to 120

Lesson 2.7   Comparing 2-Digit Numbers

You can break each number down into tens and ones to tell which number is greater.

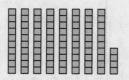   84 $<$ 88

88 has more blocks. So, 84 is less than 88.

Break each number down into tens and ones with blocks. Determine which number is greater. Write **<**, **>**, or **=** in the box.

48 ☐ 89

37 ☐ 18

Lesson 2.7 Comparing 2-Digit Numbers

You can use a number line to help you find out which number is greater and which is smaller.

77 ☐ 87

The number to the left on the number line is always smaller than the number on the right. Therefore, 77 is smaller than 87.

77 $\boxed{<}$ 87

Show each pair of numbers on a number line. Determine which number is greater. Write **<**, **>**, or **=** in the box.

1. 31 ☐ 21

2. 57 ☐ 85

Check What You Learned

Counting and Place Value

1. Color 14 mice blue. Color the rest of the mice red. Write the numbers on the lines.

_____ blue mice   _____ red mice

2. Are there more blue mice or more red mice? Use a number line to find out. Use **<**, **>**, or **=** to compare.

3. Count forward or backward. Write the 2 missing numbers. Then, draw ones and tens blocks to compare the missing numbers. Write **<**, **>**, or **=** between the blocks you draw.

54, 53, _____, 51, 50, 49, 48, _____, 46, 45

Check What You Know

Addition and Subtraction Through 20

1. Add. Draw a picture to show your thinking.

    15 + 3 = _____

2. Subtract. Use a number line to show your thinking.

    19 – 8 = _____

3. Write the number sentences for the fact family.

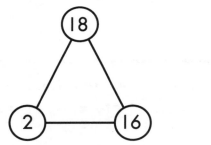

_____

_____

_____

_____

4. Turn the subtraction problem into an addition problem. Then, solve.

    20 – 14 = _____   _____ + _____ = _____

Lesson 3.1 Using Pictures to Add and Subtract

You can draw pictures to help you solve addition and subtraction problems.

7 + 4 = _____

7 + 4 = 11

14 − 6 = _____

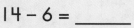 

14 − 6 = 8

Add or subtract. Draw a picture to show your thinking.

8 + 3 = _____

12 − 9 = _____

Lesson 3.2 Using a Number Line to Add and Subtract

You can use a number line to help you solve addition and subtraction problems.

7 + 4 = ?   15 − 7 = ?

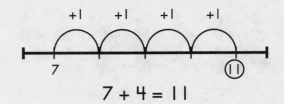   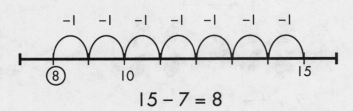

7 + 4 = 11   15 − 7 = 8

Add or subtract. Draw a number line to show your thinking.

7 + 8 = _____

13 − 4 = _____

Lesson 3.3   Using Tens and Ones to Add and Subtract

You can draw tens and ones blocks to help you add and subtract.

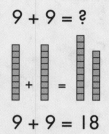

9 + 9 = ?

9 + 9 = 18

11 − 5 = ?

11 − 5 = 6

Add or subtract. Draw tens and ones blocks to show your thinking.

10 + 5 = _____

15 − 3 = _____

Lesson 3.4 Finding Unknowns

You can use different strategies to find an unknown.

Draw a number line.

$8 + ? = 12$

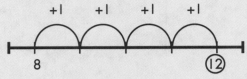

$8 + 4 = 12$

Draw a picture.

$8 + ? = 12$

$8 + 4 = 12$

Add or subtract. Draw a number line or a picture to show your thinking.

1. $13 - \underline{} = 8$

2. $\underline{} + 8 = 20$

Lesson 3.5 Addition and Subtraction Equations

Match the given equations on the right with a picture on the left.

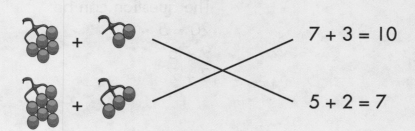

7 + 3 = 10

5 + 2 = 7

Match the pictures on the left with the equations on the right. Then, solve the equations.

7 + 9 = _____

15 − 8 = _____

9 + 9 = _____

20 − 4 = _____

Lesson 3.5   Addition and Subtraction Equations

There are multiple ways to add or subtract and get the same answer.

The answer is:
15

The question can be:
20 – 5
9 + 6
8 + 7

Write 3 different ways to add or subtract and get the number given.

20

18

9

11

Lesson 3.5 Addition and Subtraction Equations

Match the number lines on the left with the equations on the right. Then, solve the equations.

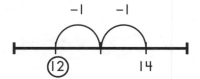

$9 + 3 =$ _____

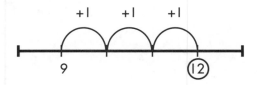

$19 - 3 =$ _____

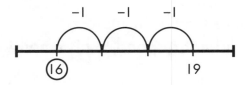

$14 - 2 =$ _____

Lesson 3.6   Addition and Subtraction in the Real World

Tyrone caught 11 fish one day. The next day, he caught 9 more fish. He cooked 4 fish for dinner that night. How many fish were left?

First day: 🐟🐟🐟🐟🐟🐟🐟🐟🐟🐟🐟
Second day: 🐟🐟🐟🐟🐟🐟🐟🐟🐟
Cross out 4 fish and count how many are left.
Tyrone has 16 fish left.

Solve each problem. Draw a picture to show your thinking.

1. A gardener planted 7 flowers in one row. He planted 12 flowers in another row. In the springtime only 13 of the flowers grew. How many flowers did not grow?

2. Nassim wrote 10 emails on Monday. He wrote 6 more emails on Tuesday. Nassim got 12 responses to his emails. How many did not respond to his emails?

Lesson 3.6   Addition and Subtraction in the Real World

Jan had 4 dolls. She lost 2 of them. Jan's grandmother bought her 4 more dolls. How many dolls does Jan have now?

Start a number line with the 4 dolls Jan began with.
Count backward by the 2 dolls she lost.
Count forward by the 4 dolls her grandmother bought her.

Jan has 6 dolls now.

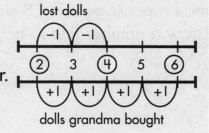

Solve each problem. Draw a number line to show your thinking.

Mischa buys 12 gallons of lemonade. She serves 9 gallons of lemonade at a party. How many gallons of lemonade are left? How much more lemonade should Mischa make to have 12 gallons for her next party?

James has 18 apples. He gives away 3 apples. He needs 20 apples to make homemade apple butter for his family. How many more apples does James need?

Lesson 3.6　Addition and Subtraction in the Real World

Solve each problem.

Jack bought 16 stamps. He mailed 10 letters and used 10 stamps. Now, he needs to mail a package using 8 stamps. Will he have enough stamps to mail his package? Draw a number line to help you solve.

Leo picks 13 peaches. Then, he picks 4 more peaches. Once he gets the peaches home, he notices that 9 of the peaches are rotten. How many peaches are still good? Can Leo make peach jam that calls for 10 fresh peaches? Draw a picture to help you solve.

Lesson 3.7 Fact Families though 20

A fact family is a collection of related addition or subtraction facts made from the same numbers.

You can use objects or drawings to help solve the problems.

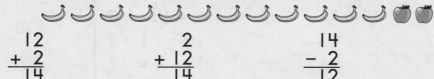

$$
\begin{array}{r} 12 \\ + 2 \\ \hline 14 \end{array}
\qquad
\begin{array}{r} 2 \\ + 12 \\ \hline 14 \end{array}
\qquad
\begin{array}{r} 14 \\ - 2 \\ \hline 12 \end{array}
\qquad
\begin{array}{r} 14 \\ - 12 \\ \hline 2 \end{array}
$$

Add or subtract. Draw a picture to show your thinking.

$$
\begin{array}{r} 19 \\ + 1 \\ \hline \end{array}
\qquad
\begin{array}{r} 1 \\ + 19 \\ \hline \end{array}
\qquad
\begin{array}{r} 20 \\ - 19 \\ \hline \end{array}
\qquad
\begin{array}{r} 20 \\ - 1 \\ \hline \end{array}
$$

$$
\begin{array}{r} 15 \\ + 3 \\ \hline \end{array}
\qquad
\begin{array}{r} 3 \\ + 15 \\ \hline \end{array}
\qquad
\begin{array}{r} 18 \\ - 3 \\ \hline \end{array}
\qquad
\begin{array}{r} 18 \\ - 15 \\ \hline \end{array}
$$

Lesson 3.7   Fact Families though 20

You can create your own fact families by choosing 2 numbers to add together. Then, you can write 4 number sentences that are true for that fact family.

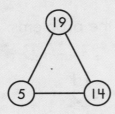

$$14 + 5 = 19$$
$$5 + 14 = 19$$
$$19 - 14 = 5$$
$$19 - 5 = 14$$

Create your own fact family triangles. Write the addition and subtraction sentences that go with each family.

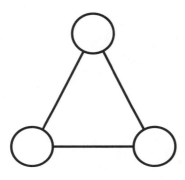

_____

_____

_____

_____

_____

_____

_____

_____

Lesson 3.8 Using Addition for Subtraction through 20

To solve the problem 15 − 12, turn it into an addition problem: 12 + ? = 15

Draw 12 objects. Then, draw and count on more objects until you reach the total of 15.

13   14   15

It took 3 more shoes to make 15. So, 12 + 3 = 15. Therefore, 15 − 12 = 3.

Add or subtract. Draw a picture to show your thinking.

19 − 7 = _____   7 + _____ = 19

12 − 1 = _____   1 + _____ = 12.

Lesson 3.8 Using Addition for Subtraction through 20

Think addition for subtraction. Solve each problem. Draw a picture to show your thinking.

16 − 13 = _____   13 + _____ = 16

---

20 − 11 = _____   11 + _____ = 20

---

18 − 7 = _____   7 + _____ = 18

Check What You Learned

Addition and Subtraction Through 20

1. Show how to solve the problem by drawing a picture. Then, show how to solve the problem with a number line.

18 fish are hiding in the sunken ship. 7 of the fish swim away. Then, a shark swims up and 2 more of the fish swim away. How many fish are still in the sunken ship?

2. Solve. Write the addition problem used and draw a picture to help you.

15 − 8 = _____   8 + _____ = 15

3. Use the problem above to complete the fact family triangle. Write 2 more number sentences for the fact family.

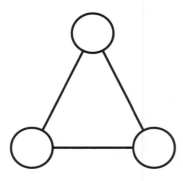

15 − 8 = 7   8 + 7 = 15
_____

_____

Mid-Test Chapters 1–3

1. Color 17 balloons red. Color 13 balloons blue.

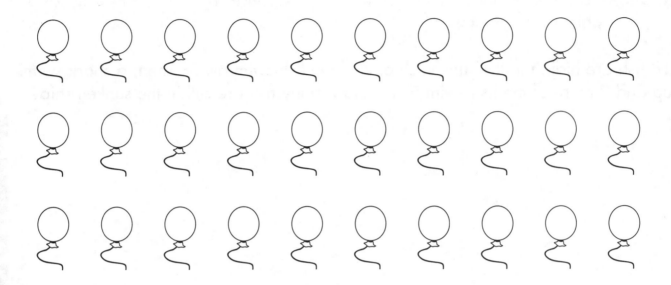

2. How many balloons are there altogether?

_____

3. How many more red balloons are there? Subtract to find the answer. Use a number line to help you solve.

Mid-Test Chapters 1–3

Solve the problems. Show your work.

4. At the apple orchard, Ella picked 6 red apples. Will picked 2 green apples. The children need 10 apples to make an apple pie. Do they have enough? Use a number line to show your work.

How many more apples do they need to pick to make a pies?

5. There were 13 books on the summer reading list. Over summer break, Ivan read 8 books. How many more books does Ivan need to read? Draw pictures to show your work.

Mid-Test   Chapters 1–3

6. Solve. Write the addition problem used. Draw a picture to help you.

14 − 4 = _____   _____ + _____ = _____

7. Use the problem above to fill out the fact family triangle. Write the 4 number sentences in the fact family.

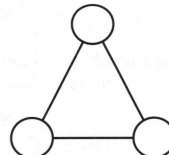

_____

_____

_____

_____

Mid-Test Chapters 1–3

Solve the problems. Show your work.

8. Bomani had 15 action figures. Lin had 12 action figures. Who had more action figures? To find out, compare the numbers using ones and tens blocks. Write **<**, **>**, or **=** between the 2 numbers.

9. Lin bought 4 more action figures. How many action figures does he have now? Use a number line to show your thinking.

NAME _____

 Check What You Know

Addition and Subtraction Through 100

CHAPTER 4 PRETEST

1. Add. Use a number line to show your thinking.

   36 + 8 =

2. Subtract. Use tens and ones blocks to show your thinking.

   80 − 40 =

Solve the problem.

3. Ginny is making holiday cards. She used 10 pieces of red paper, 6 pieces of green paper, and 2 pieces of white paper. How many pieces of paper did she use altogether? Use a number line to show your thinking.

   Write the equation used to solve the problem.

Lesson 4.1 Adding 2-Digit and 1-Digit Numbers

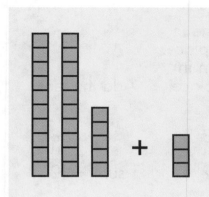

First, add ones.

Then, add tens.

$$\begin{array}{r} 25 \\ +\ 3 \\ \hline \end{array}$$

$$\begin{array}{r} 25 \\ +\ 3 \\ \hline 8 \end{array}$$

$$\begin{array}{r} 25 \\ +\ 3 \\ \hline \end{array}$$
sum = 28

Add. Draw tens and ones blocks to help you show your thinking.

$$\begin{array}{r} 27 \\ +\ 2 \\ \hline \end{array}$$

$$\begin{array}{r} 41 \\ +\ 8 \\ \hline \end{array}$$

Lesson 4.1 Adding 2-Digit and 1-Digit Numbers

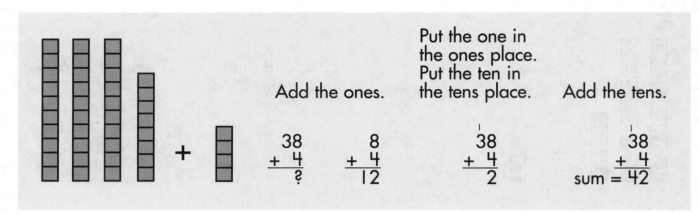

Add the ones.

38
+ 4
___
?

8
+ 4
___
12

Put the one in the ones place. Put the ten in the tens place.

38
+ 4
___
2

Add the tens.

38
+ 4
___
sum = 42

Add. Draw tens and ones blocks to help you show your thinking.

49 + 9 =

68 + 5 =

47 + 4 =

Lesson 4.1 Adding 2-Digit and 1-Digit Numbers

You can use a number line to help you add 2-digit and 1-digit numbers.

Start at the number you are given. Count on the number you are adding. The number you land on is your answer.

$16 + 3 = ?$

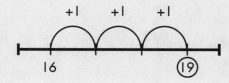

$16 + 3 = 19$

Add. Use a number line to show your thinking.

$62 + 6 =$

$73 + 8 =$

Lesson 4.1   Adding 2-Digit and 1-Digit Numbers

Add. Use a number line to show your thinking.

20 + 6 =

---

23 + 5 =

---

86 + 7 =

Lesson 4.2 Adding Multiples of 10 to 2-Digit Numbers

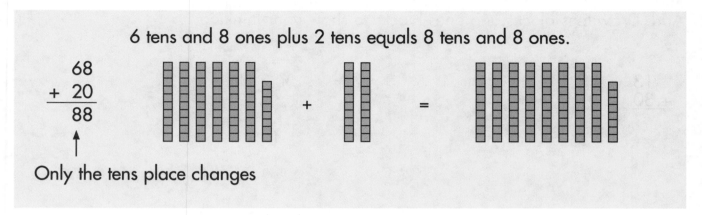

6 tens and 8 ones plus 2 tens equals 8 tens and 8 ones.

$$\begin{array}{r} 68 \\ +\ 20 \\ \hline 88 \end{array}$$

↑
Only the tens place changes

Add. Draw tens and ones blocks to show your thinking.

16 + 10 =

45 + 40 =

Lesson 4.2 Adding Multiples of 10 to 2-Digit Numbers

Add. Draw tens blocks and ones blocks to show your thinking.

```
  13
+ 30
```

```
  29
+ 50
```

```
  17
+ 60
```

Lesson 4.2 Adding Multiples of 10 to 2-Digit Numbers

You can use a number line to add multiples of 10 to 2-digit numbers.

Start at the first 2-digit number you are given. Then, count by how many tens you are adding up the number line. Where you stop is your answer.

47 + 20 = ?   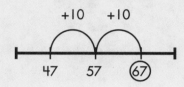   47 + 20 = 67

Add. Use a number line to show your thinking.

42 + 30 =

13 + 80 =

16 + 20 =

Lesson 4.2 Adding Multiples of 10 to 2-Digit Numbers

Add. Use a number line to show your thinking.

59 + 20 =

16 + 60 =

18 + 40 =

14 + 20 =

Lesson 4.3   Subtracting Multiples of 10

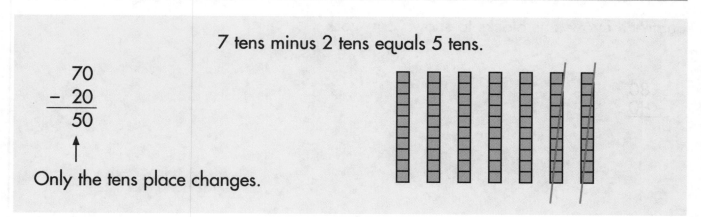

7 tens minus 2 tens equals 5 tens.

$$\begin{array}{r} 70 \\ -\ 20 \\ \hline 50 \end{array}$$

↑

Only the tens place changes.

Subtract. Draw tens blocks to show your work.

$$\begin{array}{r} 50 \\ -\ 40 \\ \hline \end{array}$$

$$\begin{array}{r} 30 \\ -\ 10 \\ \hline \end{array}$$

Lesson 4.3   Subtracting Multiples of 10

Subtract. Draw tens blocks to show your work.

$$\begin{array}{r} 80 \\ -\ 40 \\ \hline \end{array}$$

$$\begin{array}{r} 70 \\ -\ 50 \\ \hline \end{array}$$

$$\begin{array}{r} 50 \\ -\ 30 \\ \hline \end{array}$$

Lesson 4.3   Subtracting Multiples of 10

You can use a number line to subtract multiples of 10.

Start at the first number you are given. Count backward by as many tens as you are subtracting. The number you land on is your answer.

$70 - 40 = ?$

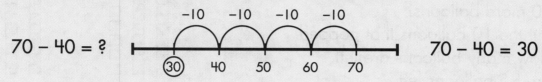

$70 - 40 = 30$

Subtract. Draw a number line to show your work.

$50 - 50 =$

$60 - 10 =$

$60 - 30 =$

Lesson 4.4 Adding and Subtracting in the Real World

There are 25 balloons at Austin's birthday party. Austin's mom blows up 30 more balloons. Then, 10 balloons pop. How many balloons are left?

Use tens and ones blocks to show 25 balloons.
Show 30 more balloons.
Cross out the 10 balloons that popped.
Count how many balloons are left.
There are 45 balloons left.

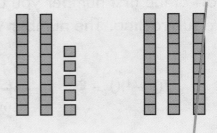

Solve the problem. Use tens and ones blocks to show your thinking.

Bailey needs 10 peaches to make 1 pie. She buys 16 peaches. James brings her 8 more peaches. Does Bailey have enough peaches to make 1 pie?

Does Bailey have enough peaches to make 2 pies?

Lesson 4.4 Adding and Subtracting in the Real World

Penny has 18 pencils to start the school year. Vanessa has 9 pencils. A new boy at school forgot his pencils. Penny and Vanessa put their pencils together and gave the boy 6 of them. How many pencils do Penny and Vanessa have left?

Use a number line to show your thinking.

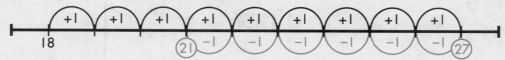

Penny and Vanessa have 21 pencils left.

Solve the problem. Draw a number line to show your thinking.

April rides 24 miles in the car to get to school. Wyatt rides 20 miles. What is the total number of miles that April and Wyatt ride to get to school?

What is the total number of miles they ride to school **and** back home?

Lesson 4.5 Adding 3 Numbers

You can draw a picture with tens and ones blocks to help you add 3 numbers.

$$\begin{array}{r} 12 \\ 4 \\ + \ 3 \\ \hline \end{array}$$ 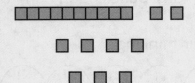 $$\begin{array}{r} 12 \\ 4 \\ + \ 3 \\ \hline 19 \end{array}$$

Add. Draw tens and ones blocks to show your thinking.

$$\begin{array}{r} 11 \\ 2 \\ + \ 6 \\ \hline \end{array}$$

$$\begin{array}{r} 5 \\ 4 \\ + \ 3 \\ \hline \end{array}$$

$$\begin{array}{r} 15 \\ 1 \\ + \ 2 \\ \hline \end{array}$$

Lesson 4.5 Adding 3 Numbers

You can use a number line to help you add 3 numbers. Start your number line at the first number in the problem. Then, count on the amount of the second number. Finally, count on the amount of the last number.
The number you land on is your answer.

$4 + 3 + 2 = ?$

$4 + 3 + 2 = 9$

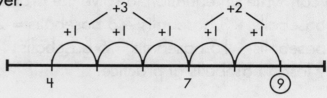

Add. Use a number line to show your thinking.

$13 + 1 + 3 =$

$17 + 1 + 2 =$

3. $5 + 5 + 3 =$

Lesson 4.6 Adding 3 Numbers in the Real World

Blair brought 11 baseballs to baseball practice. Brad brought 3, and Brianna brought 6. After practice, 15 baseballs were left. How many did they lose?

You can write an equation to solve the problem.
11 baseballs + 3 baseballs + 6 baseballs = 20 baseballs
20 baseballs − 15 baseballs = 5 baseballs
They lost 5 baseballs at practice.

Add. Write an equation to show your thinking.

The toy store sold 8 teddy bears in September, 9 in October, and 4 in November. The owner wants to sell 30 teddy bears by the end of December. How many more does the store have to sell to meet that goal?

Craig's Cupcakes sells 3 cupcakes on Sunday, 2 on Monday, and 8 on Tuesday. Last Sunday, Monday and Tuesday, the store sold a total of 15 cupcakes. Did it sell more or fewer cupcakes this week?

Lesson 4.6   Adding 3 Numbers in the Real World

Add. Write an equation to show your thinking.

Caroline ate 5 cherries, 9 grapes, and 1 banana for breakfast. How many pieces of fruit did Caroline eat in all?

_____ + _____ + _____ = _____

Caroline ate _____ pieces of fruit.

Luke ate 2 bites of potatoes, 7 bites of green beans, and 4 bites of baby carrots for dinner. How many bites did Luke eat in all?

_____ + _____ + _____ = _____

Luke ate _____ bites in all.

At the pet store, 5 guinea pigs, 9 fish, and 3 snakes are for sale. How many pets are for sale at the pet store?

_____ + _____ + _____ = _____

_____ pets are for sale at the pet store.

Check What You Learned

Addition and Subtraction Through 100

Solve the problems. Show your work.

Chase collected 26 ladybugs in one jar. He collected 10 ladybugs in a second jar. He collected 5 ladybugs in a third jar. When he checked the jars the next day, 4 ladybugs had escaped. How many ladybugs were left? Draw tens and ones blocks to show your thinking.

Write the equations used to solve the problem.

Addison had 70 nails in her tool belt. She used 20 nails to build a birdhouse. She also used 10 nails to hang the birdhouse in a tree. How many nails are left? Draw a number line to show your thinking.

Write the equation used to solve the problem.

Check What You Know

Measurement

1. Kellie drove to work at 7:00 in the morning. Write the time on the clock.

2. Leslie read a book in the park at 11:30 in the morning. Write the time on the clock.

3. Draw one object that is shorter than a spoon. Draw one object that is longer than a spoon.

Check What You Know

Measurement

4. Circle the letter next to the correct way to measure. Write the length of the object.

A.

B.

_____ dots long

Read the chart. Then, answer the questions.

Allie went to the grocery store. She counted each kind of fruit. Then, she filled out a tally chart showing the amounts of fruit she counted.

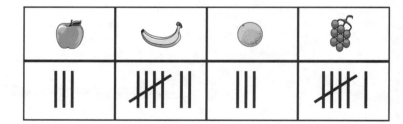

4. How many bananas and bunches of grapes did Allie count altogether? _____

5. Allie counted the same amount for 2 kinds of fruit. Which fruits were they?

_____ and _____

Lesson 5.1 Telling and Writing Time to the Hour

Read the story and the questions. Show the answers on the clocks.

Davis and Jayla have a busy day. They get up at 8:00 in the morning. Jayla packs their lunch to eat at the park. Davis gets their flying disc and soccer ball to play with. Davis and Jayla get into the car an hour after they get up. Off to the park they go! They tell Mom they will see her for dinner at 6 in the evening. Davis and Jayla will go to bed 2 hours after dinner.

What time will Davis and Jayla see Mom for dinner?

What time do Davis and Jayla get up in the morning?

What time do Davis and Jayla get into the car?

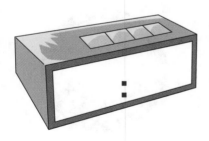

What time will Davis and Jayla go to bed?

Lesson 5.2 Telling and Writing Time to the Half Hour

Read the story and the questions. Show the answers on the clocks.

Marisa's class is going on a field trip. The bus leaves at 8:30 in the morning. It will arrive at the aquarium 1 hour later. The class will see the sharks and sting rays first. At 11:30, the class will eat lunch. A half-hour after lunch, they will watch the diving show. At 2:30 in the afternoon, Marisa's class will get on the bus to go home.

What time does Marisa get on the bus to come home?

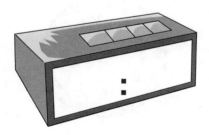

What time does Marisa's class get to the aquarium?

What time does Marisa's class watch the diving show?

What time does Marisa's bus leave in the morning?

Lesson 5.3 Ordering Objects by Size

You can put objects in order by length by comparing two objects to a third object.

The paperclip is shorter than the lollipop. The shovel is longer than the lollipop.

Draw one object that is shorter than the object given. Draw one object that is longer than the object given. Then, fill in the blanks to make each statement true.

The _____ is shorter than a pen.

The _____ is longer than a pen.

The _____ is shorter than a pitchfork.

The _____ is longer than a pitchfork.

Lesson 5.4 Comparing Lengths in the Real World

You can compare lengths of objects by telling what they are longer or shorter than.

The top pencil is longer than the middle pencil and the bottom pencil. The middle pencil is shorter than the top pencil and the bottom pencil. The bottom pencil is shorter than the top pencil, but longer than the middle pencil.

Find and draw 3 objects of different lengths. Then, fill in the blanks to tell which objects are shorter and longer.

The _____ is longer than the _____ and

_____.

The _____ is shorter than the _____ and

_____.

The _____ is shorter than the _____, but

longer than the _____.

Lesson 5.5 Measuring Length

You can measure the length of objects using smaller unit objects. The unit objects must all be the same size. They must be lined up end to end and touch each other. If the unit objects overlap or do not touch each other, the measurement will be wrong.

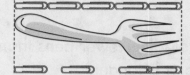

The fork is 5 paperclips long.

Circle the letter next to the correct way to measure. Write the length of each object.

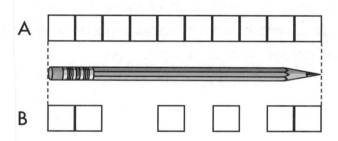

_____ squares long

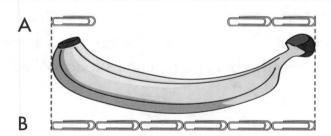

_____ paperclips long

Lesson 5.5   Measuring Length

You can use different unit objects to measure the same length.

Roberto and Rosa measure their pet snake. Roberto says the snake is 9 pens long. Rosa says the snake is 12 crayons long. Which is longer: Roberto's pen or Rosa's crayon?

9 < 12 — It takes fewer pens than crayons to measure the snake. That means Roberto's pen is longer.

Answer the questions. Use <, >, or = to compare the measurements.

First, Maya measures her desk at school with erasers. The desk is 25 erasers long. Then, she measures her desk with building blocks. The desk is 28 building blocks long. Which is longer: an eraser or a building block?

Joey measures the baseball bat with baseballs. The bat is 15 baseballs long. Marco measures the bat with pennies. The bat is 31 pennies long. Which is longer: a baseball or a penny?

Lesson 5.6 Collecting Data

Make a food chart for 1 day. Draw a picture to show how many of each type of food you ate.

Fruit   Dairy   Meat/Eggs/Fish

Vegetable   Other Foods

Breakfast	
Lunch	
Dinner	
Snacks	

Use your food chart to answer the questions.

How many of each did you eat?

Fruit _____   Dairy _____

Vegetable _____   Meats/Eggs/Fish _____

Other Foods _____

How many food items did you eat? _____

What food did you eat the most? _____

How much more fruit did you eat than vegetables? _____

Lesson 5.6   Collecting Data

Make an insect chart. Ask 10 people to tell you their favorite insect. Use tally marks to show what kind.

			Other	None

Tally Marks
$\mid$ = 1
$\mid\mid$ = 2
$\mid\mid\mid$ = 3
$\mid\mid\mid\mid$ = 4
$\cancel{\mid\mid\mid\mid}$ = 5

Use your insect chart to answer the questions.

How many people like ? _____

How many people like ? _____

How many people like ? _____

How many people do not like insects? _____

How may people like an insect that is not on the chart? _____

How many people like and ? _____

Check What You Learned

Measurement

The movie theater is screening 2 movies at 5:00 in the evening, 8 movies at 6:00, 10 movies at 7:00, and 4 movies at 8:00.

1. Organize the data into a tally chart.

5:00	6:00	7:00	8:00

2. At which time are the most movies screening? Show the answer on both clocks.

3. At which time are the fewest movies screening? Show the answer on both clocks.

4. How many movies altogether are screening at 5:00 and 8:00? _____

Check What You Learned

Measurement

Oliver, Otis, and Obie are measuring their bike ramp. Oliver says the ramp is 7 shoes long. Otis says it is 2 baseball bats long. Obie says it is 9 toy trucks long.

Fill in the blanks to tell which unit objects are shorter and longer.

5. The _____ is longer than the _____ and

_____.

6. The _____ is shorter than the _____ and

_____.

7. The _____ is shorter than the _____, but longer

than the _____.

8. Fill out a chart for the boys' unit objects. Draw pictures to show how many of each object it takes to measure the bike ramp.

Shoes	
Bats	
Trucks	

9. How many unit objects do the boys have altogether? Write the equation used to solve the problem.

Check What You Know

Geometry

1. Circle the triangle. Draw a square around the pentagon. Color the rectangle.

2. Draw a real-world example of a circle.

3. Draw a real-world example of a rectangular prism.

Spectrum Critical Thinking for Math
Grade 1

Chapter 6
Check What You Know

Check What You Know

Geometry

4. Divide the rectangle into fourths.

5. Divide the circle into halves.

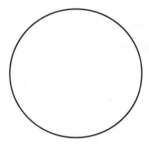

6. Shade half of the rectangle.

7. Shade one-fourth of the circle.

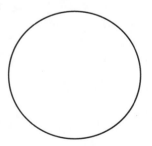

Lesson 6.1 Identifying 2-D Shapes

2-D shapes can be drawn in different ways.

The shapes below look different from each other, but they are all triangles. Triangles are 3-sided figures with 3 angles.

Draw 2 different ways to show the given shape.

Rectangle: 4 sides, 4 right angles, opposite sides are equal in length.

Square: 4 sides, 4 right angles, all sides are equal in length.

Lesson 6.2 Identifying 2-D Shapes in the Real World

You can find 2-D shapes in the real world.

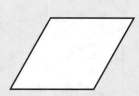   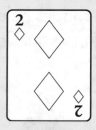

Draw 3 different real-world examples of each 2-D shape

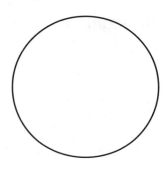

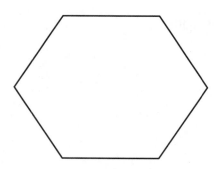

Lesson 6.3 Composing 2-D Shapes

You can compose new shapes or pictures using 2-D shapes.

rectangle   square   circle   triangle   trapezoid   pentagon   hexagon

rectangle, circle,   2 rectangles, square,   3 triangles
triangle, trapezoid   2 circles, pentagon, hexagon

Using the shapes above, compose 1 picture and 1 new shape. List the shapes you use.

Lesson 6.4 Identifying 3-D Shapes

The shapes below look different from each other, but they are all cones. Cones are solid objects with a circular flat base joined to a curved side that ends in a point.

 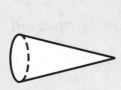  

Draw 2 different ways to show the given shape.

Cylinder: a solid object with two identical flat ends that are circular and one curved side

Cube: a solid object that is box-shaped with six identical square faces

Lesson 6.5 Identifying 3-D Shapes in the Real World

You can find 3-D shapes in the real world.

Draw 2 different ways to show each given shape.

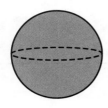

Lesson 6.6   Composing 3-D Shapes

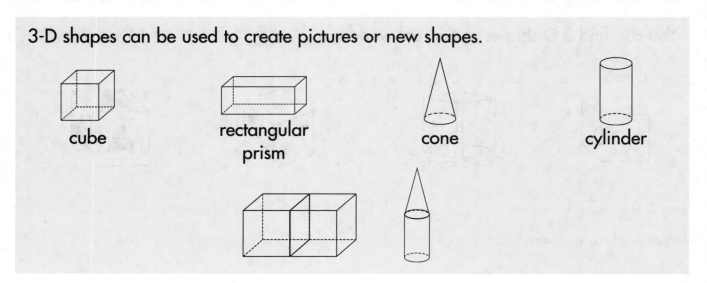

3-D shapes can be used to create pictures or new shapes.

cube   rectangular prism   cone   cylinder

Identify each 3-D shape used in the picture below.

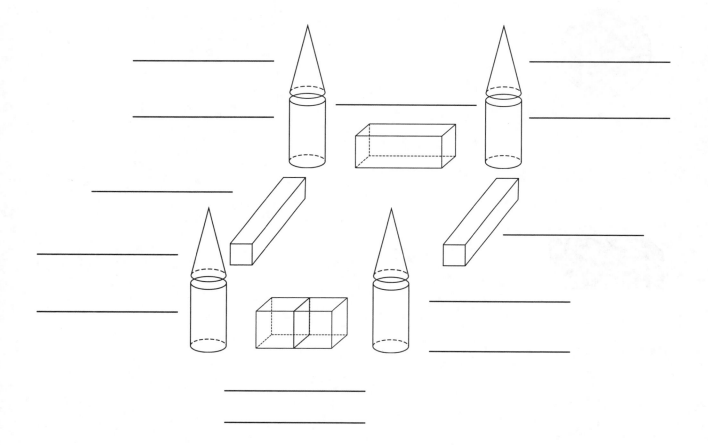

Lesson 6.7   Partitioning Circles in the Real World

A circle can be divided into equal pieces.

Draw lines to show how you and a friend can equally share the pancake.

Draw lines to show how you and 3 friends can equally share the pizza.

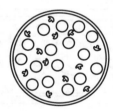

Draw 2 real-world circle pictures. Divide one into 2 equal parts. Divide the other into 4 equal parts.

Lesson 6.8 Partitioning Rectangles in the Real World

A rectangle can be divided into equal pieces.

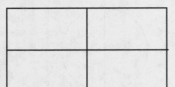 

Draw lines to show how you and a friend can equally share the gum.

Draw lines to show how you and 3 friends can equally share the soap.

Draw 2 real-world rectangle pictures. Divide one into 2 equal parts. Divide the other into 4 equal parts.

Lesson 6.9 One-Half and One-Fourth

You can show one-half of a whole and one-fourth of a whole in multiple ways.

One-half of the whole is shaded.	One-half of the whole is shaded.	One-fourth of the whole is shaded.	One-fourth of the whole is shaded.

1/2 = 1 out of 2 equal parts.	1/2 = 1 out of 2 equal parts	1/4 = 1 out of 4 equal parts	1/4 = 1 out of 4 equal parts.

Draw and shade 2 different ways to show one-fourth of a rectangle.

Draw and shade 2 different ways to show one-half of a circle.

Check What You Learned

Geometry

1. Tell what the 3 objects below have in common.

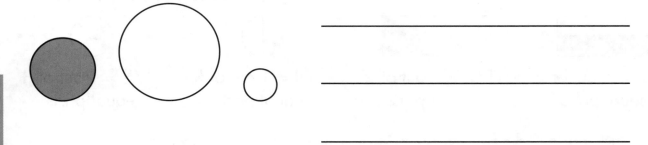

_____

_____

_____

2. Mr. Rinaldi keeps the balls for gym class in a rectangular box. Identify which 3-D shapes the box and balls are like. Then, draw each shape and combine them to create a new shape.

3. Donna baked a pan of brownies. Identify which 2-D shape Donna's pan of brownies is like. Then, draw the shape and divide it into fourths.

Check What You Learned

Geometry

4. Carter made a triangle out of 1 hexagon and 3 triangles. Draw how the triangle would look with those shapes combined.

5. Luke ate one-fourth of a rectangular pizza. After the pizza, he ate one-half of an apple pie. Draw the pizza and the pie and shade the amount of each that Luke ate.

Final Test Chapters 1–6

Solve the problems.

1. Heather and Nadia each had 20 bottles of water to give out at the race. When the race was over, Heather had 5 bottles of water left. Nadia had 6 bottles left. How many bottles of water did both girls give out during the race? Show your answer using tens and ones blocks.

2. Forrest collects 55 acorns from the backyard. Anthony collects 30 acorns. How many acorns did they collect altogether? Use a number line to show your answer.

3. Forrest and Anthony want to collect 100 acorns altogether. How many more do they need to collect? Write the equation used to solve the problem.

Final Test Chapters 1–6

Solve the problems.

4. In July, Oliver grew 30 tomatoes in his garden. He gave 20 tomatoes to a neighbor. In August, he grew 40 tomatoes. He gave 30 to a neighbor. How many tomatoes did Oliver keep for himself in July and August? Show your answer using tens blocks.

5. Did Oliver keep more tomatoes or give away more tomatoes? Compare the numbers. Write <, >, or = in the box.

_____ ☐ _____ .

6. Sam's cat had 3 baby kittens. Each kitten weighed 4 pounds. How much did the 3 kittens weigh altogether? Use a number line to show your answer.

Final Test Chapters 1–6

7. Solve. Write the addition problem used.

9 – 3 = _____   _____ + _____ = _____

8. Use the problem above to fill out the fact family triangle. Write the 4 number sentences in the fact family.

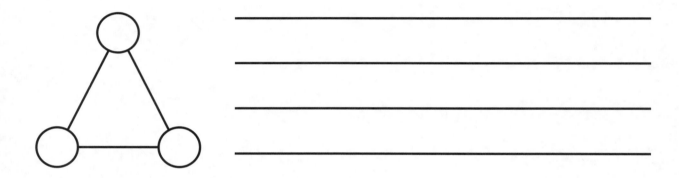

_____

_____

_____

_____

9. Follow the paths. Count forward or backward to fill in the circles.

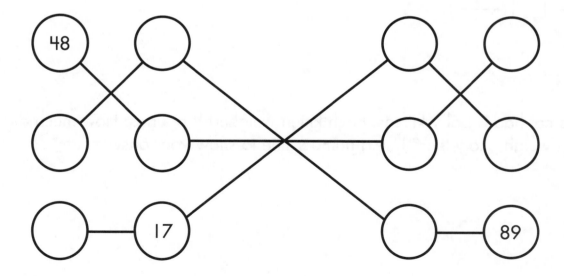

Final Test Chapters 1–6

At 3:00 in the afternoon, Rashad started counting his toys. At 3:30, he finished counting and made a chart. Look at his chart. Then, answer the questions.

Trucks	
Stuffed Animals	
Balls	
Robots	

10. How many toys does Rashad have altogether? _____

11. Does Rashad have more balls or more stuffed animals? Write each number. Then, write **<**, **>**, or **=** in the box.

_____ ☐ _____

12. How many more trucks than robots does Rashad have? Draw a picture to show your thinking.

13. Write the time Rashad started counting his toys.

14. Write the time Rashad finished counting his toys.

Final Test   Chapters 1–6

15. Circle the item that is longer than the crayon. Cross out the item that is shorter than the crayon. Draw an item that is shorter than the toothbrush but longer than the crayon.

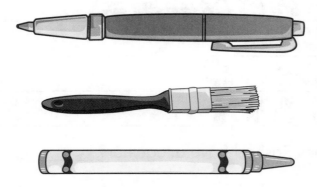

Ella is measuring her garden shovel with different unit objects.

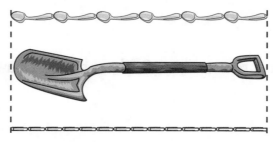

16. How many spoons long is the shovel? _____

17. How many paperclips long is the shovel? _____

18. Which is longer: a spoon or a paperclip? Write **<**, **>**, or **=** in the box.

CHAPTERS 1–6 FINAL TEST

Spectrum Critical Thinking for Math
Grade 1
100

Chapters 1–6
Final Test

Final Test Chapters 1–6

19. Lian cleaned out her backpack. She found a quarter, an envelope, a marble, and a building block. Write the shape name of each object. Draw each shape next to the shape name.

Quarter _____

Envelope _____

Marble _____

Building block _____

20. Yesterday, Cory packed a rectangular candy bar for a snack. He wanted to divide it so he and 3 friends could each have an equal piece. Draw how he divided the candy bar.

21. Today, Cory packed a donut. He wanted to divide it so he and 1 other friend could both have an equal piece. Draw how he divided the donut.

Spectrum Critical Thinking for Math
Grade 1

Chapters 1–6
Final Test
101

CHAPTERS 1–6 FINAL TEST

Answer Key

Page 4

NAME _____

Check What You Know

Addition and Subtraction Through 10

Add or subtract. Draw a picture to show your thinking.

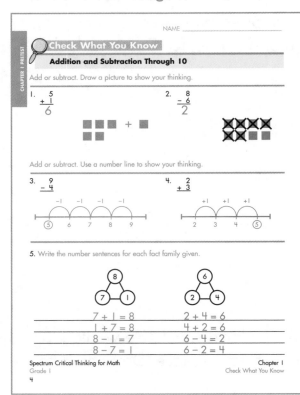

1. $5 + 1 = 6$

2. $8 - 6 = 2$

Add or subtract. Use a number line to show your thinking.

3. $9 - 4$

4. $2 + 3$

5. Write the number sentences for each fact family given.

$7 + 1 = 8$
$1 + 7 = 8$
$8 - 1 = 7$
$8 - 7 = 1$

$2 + 4 = 6$
$4 + 2 = 6$
$6 - 4 = 2$
$6 - 2 = 4$

Page 5

NAME _____

Check What You Know

Addition and Subtraction Through 10

Solve the problem below and show your work.

6. Jenny has 6 pennies. Her brother gives her 2 more pennies. When Jenny goes to the store, she wants to buy a juice box that costs 7 cents. Will Jenny be able to buy the juice box? Explain how you know. Draw a picture to help you solve.

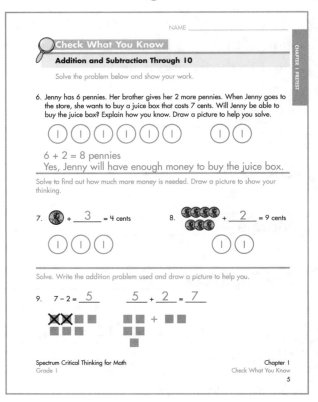

$6 + 2 = 8$ pennies
Yes, Jenny will have enough money to buy the juice box.

Solve to find out how much more money is needed. Draw a picture to show your thinking.

7. ◯ + __3__ = 4 cents

8. (coins) + __2__ = 9 cents

Solve. Write the addition problem used and draw a picture to help you.

9. $7 - 2 = $ __5__   __5__ + __2__ = __7__

Page 6

NAME _____

Lesson 1.1 Using Pictures to Add

To add 4 + 2, start by drawing four objects. Then, draw two different objects. Count the objects you have drawn altogether. The number you count is the total.

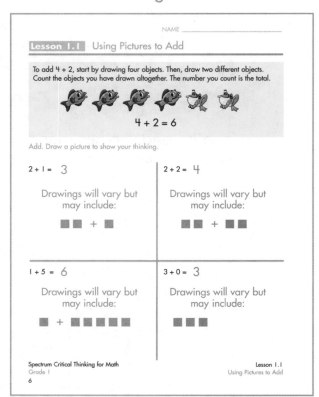

$4 + 2 = 6$

Add. Draw a picture to show your thinking.

$2 + 1 = $ 3

Drawings will vary but may include:

$2 + 2 = $ 4

Drawings will vary but may include:

$1 + 5 = $ 6

Drawings will vary but may include:

$3 + 0 = $ 3

Drawings will vary but may include:

Page 7

NAME _____

Lesson 1.2 Using Pictures to Subtract

To subtract 5 - 2, start by drawing five objects. Then, cross out the number of objects you are subtracting. Count the objects you have not crossed out. The number you have left is the difference.

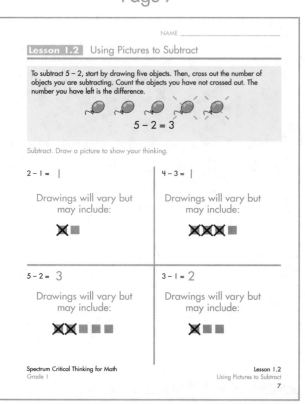

$5 - 2 = 3$

Subtract. Draw a picture to show your thinking.

$2 - 1 = $ 1

Drawings will vary but may include:

$4 - 3 = $ 1

Drawings will vary but may include:

$5 - 2 = $ 3

Drawings will vary but may include:

$3 - 1 = $ 2

Drawings will vary but may include:

Answer Key

Page 8

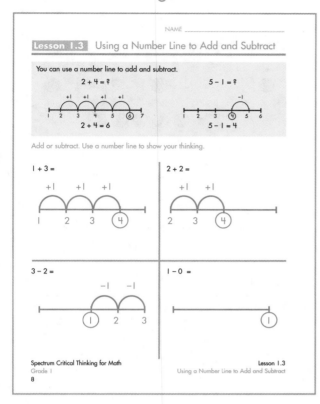

Page 9

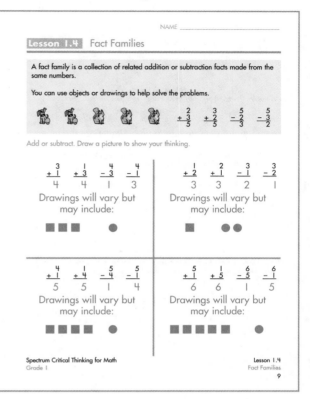

Page 10

NAME _____

Lesson 1.4 Fact Families

You can create your own fact family. Choose two numbers to add together. Then, you can write four number sentences that are true for that fact family.

$$\begin{aligned} 8 - 3 &= 5 \\ 8 - 5 &= 3 \end{aligned} \rightarrow \quad \leftarrow \left\{ \begin{aligned} 5 + 3 &= 8 \\ 3 + 5 &= 8 \end{aligned} \right.$$

Create your own fact family triangles. Write the addition and subtraction sentences that go with each family.

Answers will vary, but must include 3 numbers that fit the fact family definition, plus addition and subtraction sentences that go with each family.

Answers will vary, but must include 3 numbers that fit the fact family definition, plus addition and subtraction sentences that go with each family.

Page 11

NAME _____

Lesson 1.5 Addition in the Real World

When reading a problem, look for these keywords that tell you to add.

Addition Keywords
add   altogether   both   more   all   total   sum

Solve the problems and show your work. Circle the keywords in the problem that tell you to add.

Fuji has 4 dolls. Ana has 3 dolls. They can only fit 6 dolls in their doll carriage. Will all the dolls fit?

$4 + 3 = 7$
No, all the dolls will not fit. Fuji and Ana have 7 dolls, which is more than the carriage will hold.

Betsy has 6 pink flowers. Drew has 1 pink flower. If Drew picks 1 more flower, will they have enough to make a bouquet with a total of 10 pink flowers?

$6 + 1 = 7; 7 + 1 = 8$
No, they will not have enough. Betsy and Drew have 7 flowers. If Drew picks 1 more flower, they will only have 8 flowers.

Answer Key

Page 12

NAME

Lesson 1.6 Subtraction in the Real World

When reading a problem, look for these keywords that tell you to subtract.

Subtraction Keywords

difference | fewer | how many/much more | left | less | minus | remains | away

Solve the problems and show your work. Circle the keywords in the problem that tell you to subtract.

There are 8 cars in the parking lot. 2 cars drive away. Then, 5 more drive away. How many cars are left in the parking lot?

8 − 2 = 6; 6 − 5 = 1
There is 1 car left in the parking lot.

Tia and Dante bought 10 apples to make an apple cobbler. Tia peeled 5 of the apples. Dante peeled 2. How many apples are left to peel?

10 − 5 = 5; 5 − 2 = 3
There are 3 apples left to peel.

Spectrum Critical Thinking for Math
Grade 1
12

Lesson 1.6
Subtraction in the Real World

Page 13

NAME

Lesson 1.7 Adding with Coins

1 penny — 1¢   1 nickel — 5¢   1 dime — 10¢

5 pennies
5 cents

Add the amounts together and write how much money. Draw the coins to show your thinking.

2 pennies, 1 nickel

1 + 1 = 2; 2 + 5 = 7

__7__ cents   (1) (1) (5)

2 nickels

5 + 5 = 10

__10__ cents   (5) (5)

1 nickel, 3 pennies

1 + 1 = 2; 2 + 1 = 3; 3 + 5 = 8

__8__ cents   (5) (1) (1) (1)

Spectrum Critical Thinking for Math
Grade 1

Lesson 1.7
Adding with Coins
13

Page 14

NAME

Lesson 1.7 Adding with Coins

How much more money is needed to reach the total?

4 pennies = 4 cents. Count on from 4 to determine how much more money is needed.

+ ? = 8 cents

? = . Four more pennies are needed to make 8 cents.

Solve to find out how much more money is needed. Draw a picture to show your thinking.

+ __4__ = 9 cents

(1) (1) (1) (1)

+ __3__ = 6 cents

(1) (1) (1)

Spectrum Critical Thinking for Math
Grade 1
14

Lesson 1.7
Adding with Coins

Page 15

NAME

Lesson 1.8 Coins in the Real World

John has 3 pennies. Ana has 2 pennies. How much money do they have altogether?

Drawing a picture can help you solve the problem.

+ =

John and Ana have 5 pennies altogether.

Solve the problems. Show your work.

Victor has 2 pennies. Then, he finds 6 more pennies. Can he buy a piece of candy that costs 7 cents? Explain how you know.

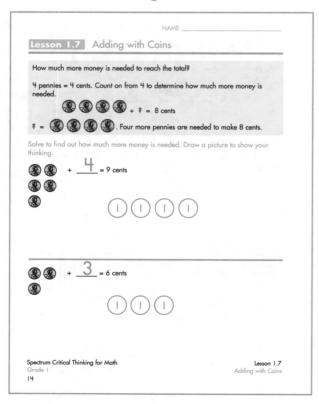

(1) (1) + (1) (1) (1) (1) (1) (1)

= (1) (1) (1) (1) (1) (1) (1) (1)

Yes. He can buy a piece of candy that costs 7 cents because he has 8 cents.

Lin has 5 pennies. Barb has 6 cents. Lin says she has the same amount of money as Barb, but Barb disagrees. Who is correct? Explain how you know.

Lin: (1) (1) (1) (1) (1)

Barb: (1) (1) (1) (1) (1) (1)

Barb is correct because 5 pennies is 5 cents, and 6 cents is 6 pennies.

Spectrum Critical Thinking for Math
Grade 1
15

Lesson 1.8
Coins in the Real World

Answer Key

Page 16

Lesson 1.9 Using Addition for Subtraction

To solve the problem 8 – 4, turn it into an addition problem: 4 + ? = 8.

Draw 4 objects. Then, draw and count on more objects until you reach the total of 8.

Solve. Write the addition problem used and draw a picture to help you.

$10 - 3 = \underline{7}$ $\underline{3} + \underline{7} = \underline{10}$

Drawings will vary but may include:

$8 - 2 = \underline{6}$ $\underline{2} + \underline{6} = \underline{8}$

Drawings will vary but may include:

$7 - 2 = \underline{5}$ $\underline{2} + \underline{5} = \underline{7}$

Drawings will vary but may include:

Page 17

Lesson 1.9 Using Addition for Subtraction

To solve the problem 9 – 7, turn it into an addition problem: 7 + ? = 9.

Draw 7 tally marks. Then, draw and count on more tallies until you reach the total of 9.

It took 2 more tally marks to make 9. So, 7 + 2 = 9, and 9 – 7 = 2.

Solve. Write the addition problem used and draw tally marks to help you.

$5 - 1 = \underline{4}$ $\underline{1} + \underline{4} = \underline{5}$

Drawings will vary but may include:

$10 - 4 = \underline{6}$ $\underline{4} + \underline{6} = \underline{10}$

Drawings will vary but may include:

$8 - 5 = \underline{3}$ $\underline{3} + \underline{5} = \underline{8}$

Drawings will vary but may include:

Page 18

💡 **Check What You Learned**

Addition and Subtraction Through 10

Add or subtract. Draw a picture to show your thinking.

1. $\begin{array}{r} 8 \\ -\ 4 \\ \hline 4 \end{array}$ 2. $\begin{array}{r} 3 \\ +\ 4 \\ \hline 7 \end{array}$

Add or subtract. Use a number line to show your thinking.

3. $\begin{array}{r} 8 \\ +\ 1 \\ \hline 9 \end{array}$ 4. $\begin{array}{r} 9 \\ -\ 6 \\ \hline 3 \end{array}$

5. Jasmine has 3 pennies. Marcus has 1 nickel. How much money do they have altogether? Draw a picture to help you solve.

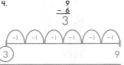

$= 8¢$ altogether

CHAPTER 1 POSTTEST

Page 19

💡 **Check What You Learned**

Addition and Subtraction Through 10

Solve the problem and show your work.

6. Jan had 4 dolls sitting on a shelf. The dog ran off with 2 of the dolls. Jan was able to find 1 of the dolls outside in the doghouse. How many dolls does Jan have now?

$4 - 2 = 2$ subtract the dolls the dog took
$2 + 1 = 3$ add the one she found

Jan has 3 dolls now.

Solve. Write the addition problem used and draw a picture to help you. Then, fill out the fact family triangle. Use the triangle to write one more addition problem and one more subtraction problem.

7. $7 - 5 = \underline{2}$ $\underline{2} + \underline{5} = \underline{7}$

$\underline{7} - \underline{2} = \underline{5}$ $\underline{5} + \underline{2} = \underline{7}$

CHAPTER 1 POSTTEST

Answer Key

Page 20

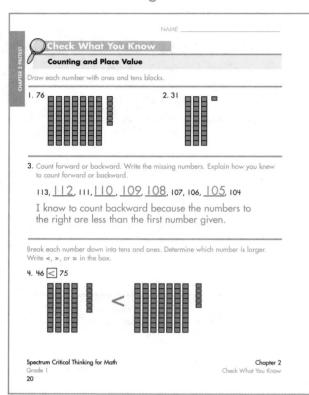

Check What You Know

Counting and Place Value

Draw each number with ones and tens blocks.

1. 76

2. 31

3. Count forward or backward. Write the missing numbers. Explain how you knew to count forward or backward.

113, 112, 111, 110, 109, 108, 107, 106, 105, 104

I know to count backward because the numbers to the right are less than the first number given.

Break each number down into tens and ones. Determine which number is larger. Write <, >, or = in the box.

4. 46 < 75

Page 21

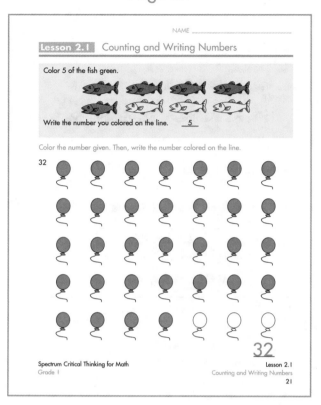

Lesson 2.1 Counting and Writing Numbers

Color 5 of the fish green.

Write the number you colored on the line.   5

Color the number given. Then, write the number colored on the line.

32

32

Page 22

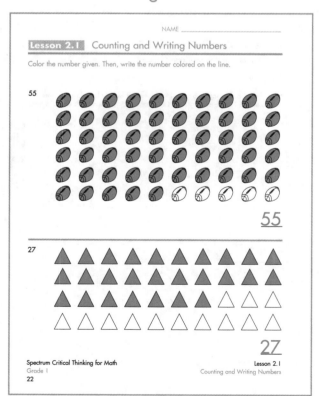

Lesson 2.1 Counting and Writing Numbers

Color the number given. Then, write the number colored on the line.

55

55

27

27

Page 23

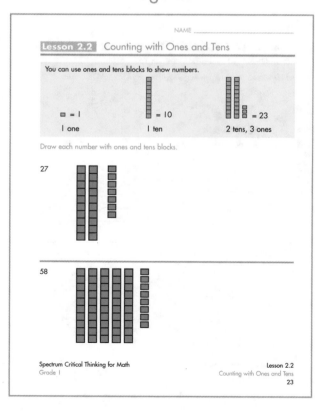

Lesson 2.2 Counting with Ones and Tens

You can use ones and tens blocks to show numbers.

□ = 1
1 one

= 10
1 ten

= 23
2 tens, 3 ones

Draw each number with ones and tens blocks.

27

58

Answer Key

Page 24

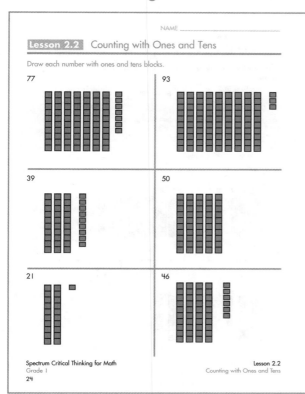

NAME _____

Lesson 2.2 Counting with Ones and Tens

Draw each number with ones and tens blocks.

77   93

39   50

21   46

Page 25

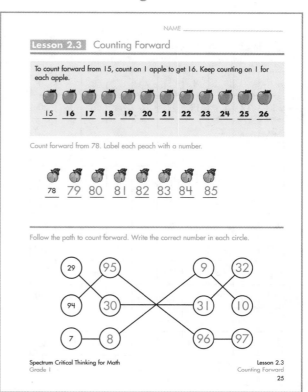

NAME _____

Lesson 2.3 Counting Forward

To count forward from 15, count on 1 apple to get 16. Keep counting on 1 for each apple.

15 **16** **17** **18** **19** **20** **21** **22** **23** **24** **25** **26**

Count forward from 78. Label each peach with a number.

78 **79** **80** **81** **82** **83** **84** **85**

Follow the path to count forward. Write the correct number in each circle.

29 95   9 32
94 30   31 10
7 8   96 97

Page 26

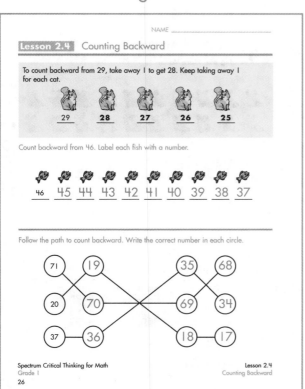

NAME _____

Lesson 2.4 Counting Backward

To count backward from 29, take away 1 to get 28. Keep taking away 1 for each cat.

29 **28** **27** **26** **25**

Count backward from 46. Label each fish with a number.

46 **45** **44** **43** **42** **41** **40** **39** **38** **37**

Follow the path to count backward. Write the correct number in each circle.

71 19   35 68
20 70   69 34
37 36   18 17

Page 27

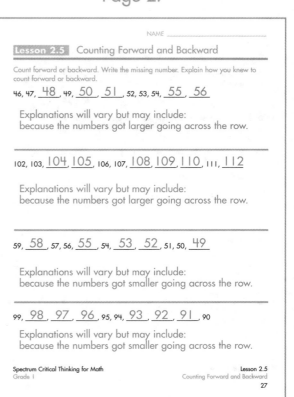

NAME _____

Lesson 2.5 Counting Forward and Backward

Count forward or backward. Write the missing number. Explain how you knew to count forward or backward.

46, 47, **48**, 49, **50**, **51**, 52, 53, 54, **55**, **56**

Explanations will vary but may include:
because the numbers got larger going across the row.

102, 103, **104**, **105**, 106, 107, **108**, **109**, **110**, 111, **112**

Explanations will vary but may include:
because the numbers got larger going across the row.

59, **58**, 57, 56, **55**, 54, **53**, **52**, 51, 50, **49**

Explanations will vary but may include:
because the numbers got smaller going across the row.

99, **98**, **97**, **96**, 95, 94, **93**, **92**, **91**, 90

Explanations will vary but may include:
because the numbers got smaller going across the row.

Answer Key

Page 28

NAME _____

Lesson 2.6 Counting to 120

Count forward. Write the missing numbers.

1	2	3	4	5	6	7	8	9	10
11	12	13	14	15	16	17	18	19	20
21	22	23	24	25	26	27	28	29	30
31	32	33	34	35	36	37	38	39	40
41	42	43	44	45	46	47	48	49	50
51	52	53	54	55	56	57	58	59	60
61	62	63	64	65	66	67	68	69	70
71	72	73	74	75	76	77	78	79	80
81	82	83	84	85	86	87	88	89	90
91	92	93	94	95	96	97	98	99	100
101	102	103	104	105	106	107	108	109	110
111	112	113	114	115	116	117	118	119	120

Page 29

NAME _____

Lesson 2.7 Comparing 2-Digit Numbers

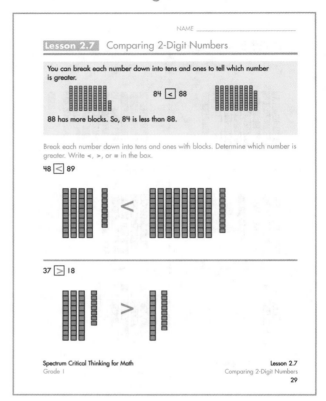

You can break each number down into tens and ones to tell which number is greater.

84 < 88

88 has more blocks. So, 84 is less than 88.

Break each number down into tens and ones with blocks. Determine which number is greater. Write <, >, or = in the box.

48 < 89

37 > 18

Page 30

NAME _____

Lesson 2.7 Comparing 2-Digit Numbers

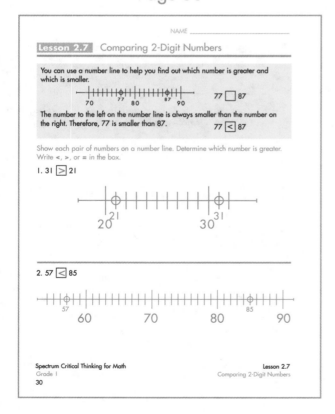

You can use a number line to help you find out which number is greater and which is smaller.

77 □ 87

The number to the left on the number line is always smaller than the number on the right. Therefore, 77 is smaller than 87.

77 < 87

Show each pair of numbers on a number line. Determine which number is greater. Write <, >, or = in the box.

1. 31 > 21

2. 57 < 85

Page 31

NAME _____

💡 **Check What You Learned**

Counting and Place Value

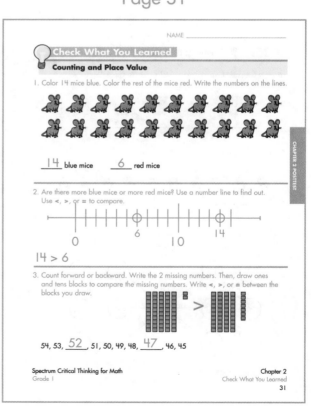

1. Color 14 mice blue. Color the rest of the mice red. Write the numbers on the lines.

__14__ blue mice   __6__ red mice

2. Are there more blue mice or more red mice? Use a number line to find out. Use <, >, or = to compare.

14 > 6

3. Count forward or backward. Write the 2 missing numbers. Then, draw ones and tens blocks to compare the missing numbers. Write <, >, or = between the blocks you draw.

54, 53, __52__, 51, 50, 49, 48, __47__, 46, 45

CHAPTER 2 POSTTEST

Answer Key

Page 32

NAME _____

CHAPTER 3 PRETEST

Check What You Know

Addition and Subtraction Through 20

1. Add. Draw a picture to show your thinking.

$15 + 3 = \underline{18}$

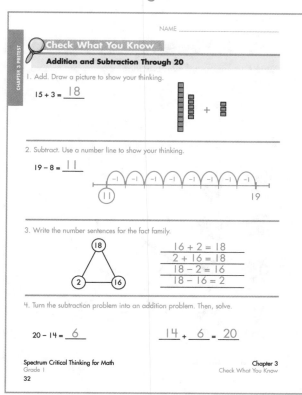

2. Subtract. Use a number line to show your thinking.

$19 - 8 = \underline{11}$

⑪ ... 19

3. Write the number sentences for the fact family.

⑱ ② ⑯

$16 + 2 = 18$
$2 + 16 = 18$
$18 - 2 = 16$
$18 - 16 = 2$

4. Turn the subtraction problem into an addition problem. Then, solve.

$20 - 14 = \underline{6}$ $\underline{14} + \underline{6} = \underline{20}$

Spectrum Critical Thinking for Math
Grade 1
32

Chapter 3
Check What You Know

Page 33

NAME _____

Lesson 3.1 Using Pictures to Add and Subtract

You can draw pictures to help you solve addition and subtraction problems.

$7 + 4 = \underline{}$ $14 - 6 = \underline{}$

$7 + 4 = 11$ $14 - 6 = 8$

Add or subtract. Draw a picture to show your thinking.

$8 + 3 = \underline{11}$

Drawings will vary but may include:

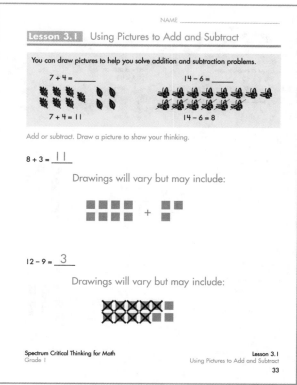

$12 - 9 = \underline{3}$

Drawings will vary but may include:

Spectrum Critical Thinking for Math
Grade 1

Lesson 3.1
Using Pictures to Add and Subtract
33

Page 34

NAME _____

Lesson 3.2 Using a Number Line to Add and Subtract

You can use a number line to help you solve addition and subtraction problems.

$7 + 4 = ?$ $15 - 7 = ?$

$7 + 4 = 11$ $15 - 7 = 8$

Add or subtract. Draw a number line to show your thinking.

$7 + 8 = \underline{15}$

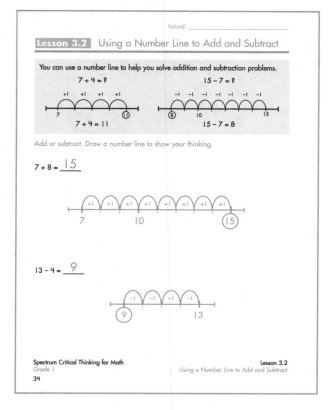

7   10   ⑮

$13 - 4 = \underline{9}$

⑨   13

Spectrum Critical Thinking for Math
Grade 1
34

Lesson 3.2
Using a Number Line to Add and Subtract

Page 35

NAME _____

Lesson 3.3 Using Tens and Ones to Add and Subtract

You can draw tens and ones blocks to help you add and subtract.

$9 + 9 = ?$ $11 - 5 = ?$

$9 + 9 = 18$ $11 - 5 = 6$

Add or subtract. Draw tens and ones blocks to show your thinking.

$10 + 5 = \underline{15}$

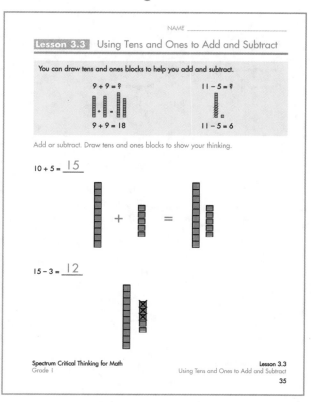

$15 - 3 = \underline{12}$

Spectrum Critical Thinking for Math
Grade 1

Lesson 3.3
Using Tens and Ones to Add and Subtract
35

Answer Key

Page 36

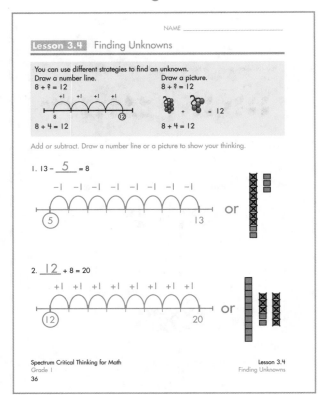

Lesson 3.4 Finding Unknowns

You can use different strategies to find an unknown.
Draw a number line.
$8 + ? = 12$

$8 + 4 = 12$

Draw a picture.
$8 + ? = 12$

$8 + 4 = 12$

Add or subtract. Draw a number line or a picture to show your thinking.

1. $13 - \underline{5} = 8$

or

2. $\underline{12} + 8 = 20$

or

Page 37

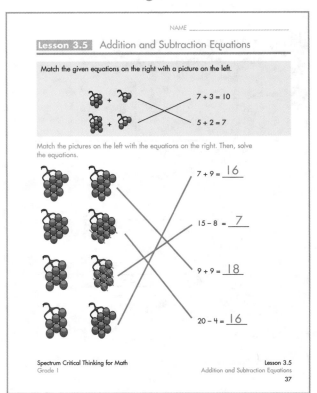

Lesson 3.5 Addition and Subtraction Equations

Match the given equations on the right with a picture on the left.

$7 + 3 = 10$

$5 + 2 = 7$

Match the pictures on the left with the equations on the right. Then, solve the equations.

$7 + 9 = \underline{16}$

$15 - 8 = \underline{7}$

$9 + 9 = \underline{18}$

$20 - 4 = \underline{16}$

Page 38

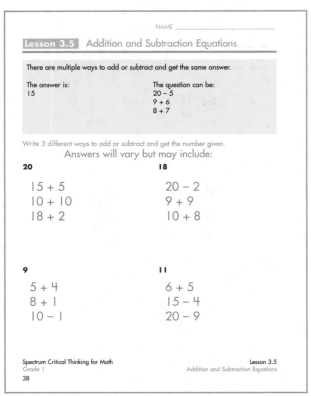

Lesson 3.5 Addition and Subtraction Equations

There are multiple ways to add or subtract and get the same answer.

The answer is:
15

The question can be:
$20 - 5$
$9 + 6$
$8 + 7$

Write 3 different ways to add or subtract and get the number given.

Answers will vary but may include:

20

$15 + 5$
$10 + 10$
$18 + 2$

18

$20 - 2$
$9 + 9$
$10 + 8$

9

$5 + 4$
$8 + 1$
$10 - 1$

11

$6 + 5$
$15 - 4$
$20 - 9$

Page 39

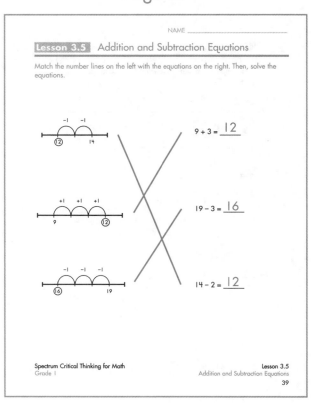

Lesson 3.5 Addition and Subtraction Equations

Match the number lines on the left with the equations on the right. Then, solve the equations.

$9 + 3 = \underline{12}$

$19 - 3 = \underline{16}$

$14 - 2 = \underline{12}$

Answer Key

Page 40

NAME _____

Lesson 3.6 Addition and Subtraction in the Real World

Tyrone caught 11 fish one day. The next day, he caught 9 more fish. He cooked 4 fish for dinner that night. How many fish were left?

First day: 🐟🐟🐟🐟🐟🐟🐟🐟🐟🐟🐟
Second day: 🐟🐟🐟🐟🐟🐟🐟🐟🐟
Cross out 4 fish and count how many are left.
Tyrone has 16 fish left.

Solve each problem. Draw a picture to show your thinking.

1. A gardener planted 7 flowers in one row. He planted 12 flowers in another row. In the springtime only 13 of the flowers grew. How many flowers did not grow?

$7 + 12 = $ ▯▯▯▯▯▯▯ + ▯▯▯▯▯▯▯▯▯▯ ▯▯ $= 19$
$19 - 13 = $ ▨▨▨▨▨▨▨ ▨▨▨▨▨▨ $= 6$

6 flowers did not grow.

2. Nassim wrote 10 emails on Monday. He wrote 6 more emails on Tuesday. Nassim got 12 responses to his emails. How many did not respond to his emails?

$10 + 6 = $ ▨▨▨▨▨▨▨▨▨▨ + ▯▯▯▯▯▯ $= 16$
$16 - 12 = $ ▨▨▨▨▨▨ ▨▨▯▯▯▯ $= 4$

4 did not respond to Nassim's emails.

Page 41

NAME _____

Lesson 3.6 Addition and Subtraction in the Real World

Jan had 4 dolls. She lost 2 of them. Jan's grandmother bought her 4 more dolls. How many dolls does Jan have now?

Start a number line with the 4 dolls Jan began with. Count backward by the 2 dolls she lost. Count forward by the 4 dolls her grandmother bought her.

Jan has 6 dolls now.

Solve each problem. Draw a number line to show your thinking.

Mischa buys 12 gallons of lemonade. She serves 9 gallons of lemonade at a party. How many gallons of lemonade are left? How much more lemonade should Mischa make to have 12 gallons for her next party?

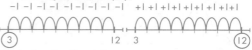

Mischa has 3 gallons left.
Mischa would have to make 9 more gallons.

James has 18 apples. He gives away 3 apples. He needs 20 apples to make homemade apple butter for his family. How many more apples does James need?

James will need 5 more apples.

Page 42

NAME _____

Lesson 3.6 Addition and Subtraction in the Real World

Solve each problem.

Jack bought 16 stamps. He mailed 10 letters and used 10 stamps. Now, he needs to mail a package using 8 stamps. Will he have enough stamps to mail his package? Draw a number line to help you solve.

Jack will not have enough stamps. He will only have 6 stamps left after he mails his letters, and he needs 8.

$16 - 10 = 6$

Leo picks 13 peaches. Then, he picks 4 more peaches. Once he gets the peaches home, he notices that 9 of the peaches are rotten. How many peaches are still good? Can Leo make peach jam that calls for 10 fresh peaches? Draw a picture to help you solve.

When Leo gets home, 8 of the peaches are still good. He cannot make peach jam. He needs 10 peaches, and he only has 8.

Page 43

NAME _____

Lesson 3.7 Fact Families though 20

A fact family is a collection of related addition or subtraction facts made from the same numbers.

You can use objects or drawings to help solve the problems.

🍌🍌🍌🍌🍌🍌🍌🍌🍌🍌🍌🍌🍌🍌

$\begin{array}{r}12\\+2\\\hline14\end{array}$ $\begin{array}{r}2\\+12\\\hline14\end{array}$ $\begin{array}{r}14\\-2\\\hline12\end{array}$ $\begin{array}{r}14\\-12\\\hline2\end{array}$

Add or subtract. Draw a picture to show your thinking.

$\begin{array}{r}19\\+1\\\hline20\end{array}$ $\begin{array}{r}1\\+19\\\hline20\end{array}$ $\begin{array}{r}20\\-19\\\hline1\end{array}$ $\begin{array}{r}20\\-1\\\hline19\end{array}$

Drawings will vary but may include:

$\begin{array}{r}15\\+3\\\hline18\end{array}$ $\begin{array}{r}3\\+15\\\hline18\end{array}$ $\begin{array}{r}18\\-3\\\hline15\end{array}$ $\begin{array}{r}18\\-15\\\hline3\end{array}$

Drawings will vary but may include:

Answer Key

Page 44

Lesson 3.7 Fact Families though 20

You can create your own fact families by choosing 2 numbers to add together. Then, you can write 4 number sentences that are true for that fact family.

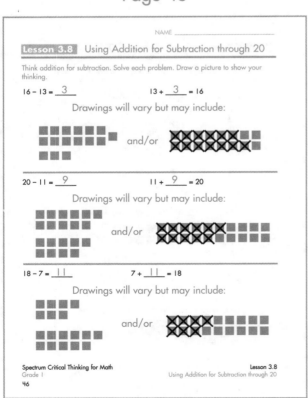

$14 + 5 = 19$
$5 + 14 = 19$
$19 - 14 = 5$
$19 - 5 = 14$

Create your own fact family triangles. Write the addition and subtraction sentences that go with each family.

Answers will vary for each question but should include 3 numbers that make up a fact family.

Page 45

Lesson 3.8 Using Addition for Subtraction through 20

To solve the problem $15 - 12$, turn it into an addition problem: $12 + ? = 15$

Draw 12 objects. Then, draw and count on more objects until you reach the total of 15.

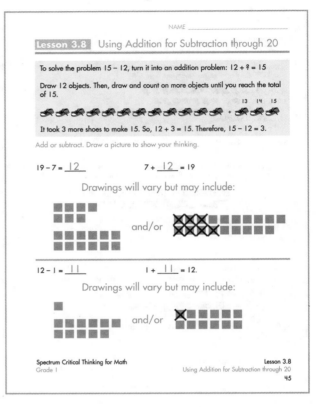

It took 3 more shoes to make 15. So, $12 + 3 = 15$. Therefore, $15 - 12 = 3$.

Add or subtract. Draw a picture to show your thinking.

$19 - 7 = \underline{12}$ $7 + \underline{12} = 19$

Drawings will vary but may include:

and/or

$12 - 1 = \underline{11}$ $1 + \underline{11} = 12$.

Drawings will vary but may include:

and/or

Page 46

Lesson 3.8 Using Addition for Subtraction through 20

Think addition for subtraction. Solve each problem. Draw a picture to show your thinking.

$16 - 13 = \underline{3}$ $13 + \underline{3} = 16$

Drawings will vary but may include:

and/or

$20 - 11 = \underline{9}$ $11 + \underline{9} = 20$

Drawings will vary but may include:

and/or

$18 - 7 = \underline{11}$ $7 + \underline{11} = 18$

Drawings will vary but may include:

and/or

Page 47

Check What You Learned

Addition and Subtraction Through 20

1. Show how to solve the problem by drawing a picture. Then, show how to solve the problem with a number line.

18 fish are hiding in the sunken ship. 7 of the fish swim away. Then, a shark swims up and 2 more of the fish swim away. How many fish are still in the sunken ship?

Drawings will vary but may include:

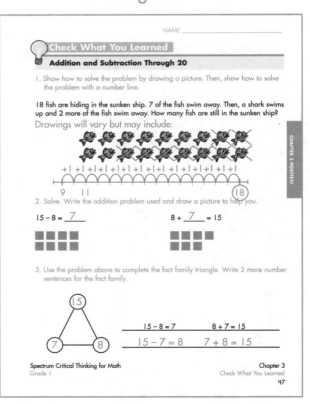

2. Solve. Write the addition problem used and draw a picture to help you.

$15 - 8 = \underline{7}$ $8 + \underline{7} = 15$

3. Use the problem above to complete the fact family triangle. Write 2 more number sentences for the fact family.

$15 - 8 = 7$ $8 + 7 = 15$
$15 - 7 = 8$ $7 + 8 = 15$

CHAPTER 3 POSTTEST

Answer Key

Page 48

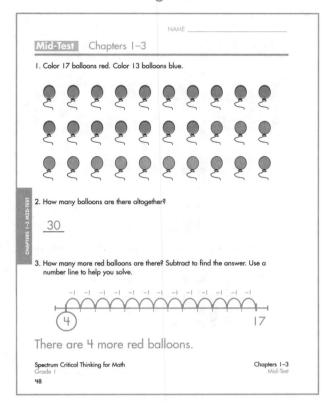

Mid-Test Chapters 1–3

1. Color 17 balloons red. Color 13 balloons blue.

2. How many balloons are there altogether?

   <u>30</u>

3. How many more red balloons are there? Subtract to find the answer. Use a number line to help you solve.

   (4) ——————————— 17

There are 4 more red balloons.

Page 49

Mid-Test Chapters 1–3

Solve the problems. Show your work.

4. At the apple orchard, Ella picked 6 red apples. Will picked 2 green apples. The children need 10 apples to make an apple pie. Do they have enough? Use a number line to show your work.

   6 → +1 +1 → (8)
   6   8

   6 + 2 = 8

They do not have enough apples to make a pie.

How many more apples do they need to pick to make a pies?

   (2) —————————————— 10

They need to pick 2 more apples.

5. There were 13 books on the summer reading list. Over summer break, Ivan read 8 books. How many more books does Ivan need to read? Draw pictures to show your work.

Drawings will vary but may include:

❌❌❌❌❌❌❌❌⬜⬜⬜⬜⬜

Ivan needs to read 5 more books.

Page 50

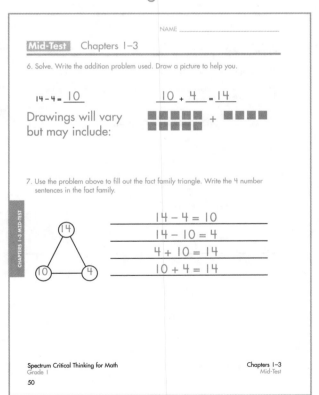

Mid-Test Chapters 1–3

6. Solve. Write the addition problem used. Draw a picture to help you.

   14 – 4 = <u>10</u>   <u>10</u> + <u>4</u> = <u>14</u>

Drawings will vary but may include:

7. Use the problem above to fill out the fact family triangle. Write the 4 number sentences in the fact family.

   (14)
   (10) (4)

   14 – 4 = 10
   14 – 10 = 4
   4 + 10 = 14
   10 + 4 = 14

Page 51

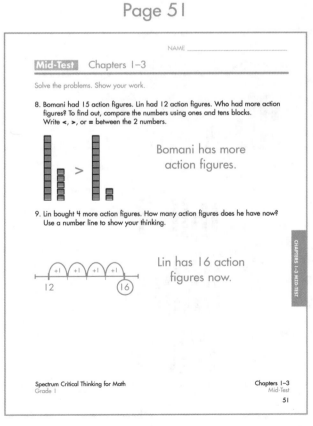

Mid-Test Chapters 1–3

Solve the problems. Show your work.

8. Bomani had 15 action figures. Lin had 12 action figures. Who had more action figures? To find out, compare the numbers using ones and tens blocks. Write <, >, or = between the 2 numbers.

   >

   Bomani has more action figures.

9. Lin bought 4 more action figures. How many action figures does he have now? Use a number line to show your thinking.

   12 +1 +1 +1 +1 (16)

   Lin has 16 action figures now.

Page 52

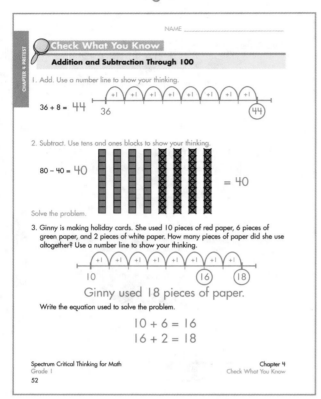

Check What You Know

Addition and Subtraction Through 100

1. Add. Use a number line to show your thinking.

$36 + 8 =$ 44

2. Subtract. Use tens and ones blocks to show your thinking.

$80 - 40 =$ 40

$= 40$

Solve the problem.

3. Ginny is making holiday cards. She used 10 pieces of red paper, 6 pieces of green paper, and 2 pieces of white paper. How many pieces of paper did she use altogether? Use a number line to show your thinking.

Ginny used 18 pieces of paper.

Write the equation used to solve the problem.

$10 + 6 = 16$
$16 + 2 = 18$

Page 53

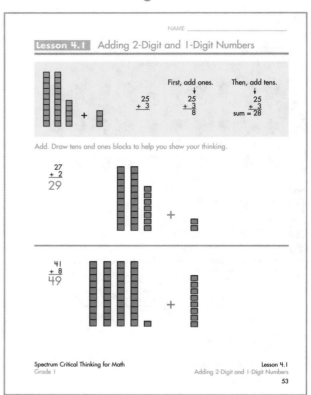

Lesson 4.1 Adding 2-Digit and 1-Digit Numbers

First, add ones.
25
$+\ 3$

Then, add tens.
25
$+\ 3$
8

25
$+\ 3$
sum = 28

Add. Draw tens and ones blocks to help you show your thinking.

27
$+\ 2$
29

41
$+\ 8$
49

Page 54

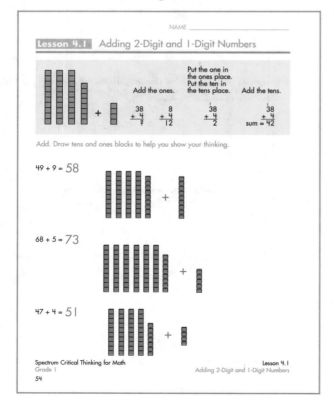

Lesson 4.1 Adding 2-Digit and 1-Digit Numbers

Add the ones.
38
$+\ 4$
$?$

8
$+\ 4$
12

Put the one in the ones place. Put the ten in the tens place.
38
$+\ 4$
2

Add the tens.
38
$+\ 4$
sum = 42

Add. Draw tens and ones blocks to help you show your thinking.

$49 + 9 =$ 58

$68 + 5 =$ 73

$47 + 4 =$ 51

Page 55

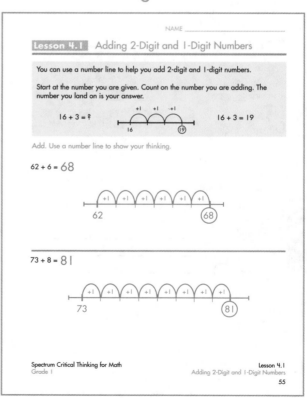

Lesson 4.1 Adding 2-Digit and 1-Digit Numbers

You can use a number line to help you add 2-digit and 1-digit numbers.

Start at the number you are given. Count on the number you are adding. The number you land on is your answer.

$16 + 3 = ?$ $16 + 3 = 19$

Add. Use a number line to show your thinking.

$62 + 6 =$ 68

$73 + 8 =$ 81

Answer Key

Page 56

NAME _____

Lesson 4.1 Adding 2-Digit and 1-Digit Numbers

Add. Use a number line to show your thinking.

$20 + 6 = 26$

20 ─── 26

$23 + 5 = 28$

23 ─── 28

$86 + 7 = 93$

86 ─── 93

Page 57

NAME _____

Lesson 4.2 Adding Multiples of 10 to 2-Digit Numbers

6 tens and 8 ones plus 2 tens equals 8 tens and 8 ones.

$\begin{array}{r} 68 \\ + 20 \\ \hline 88 \end{array}$

Only the tens place changes

Add. Draw tens and ones blocks to show your thinking.

$16 + 10 = 26$

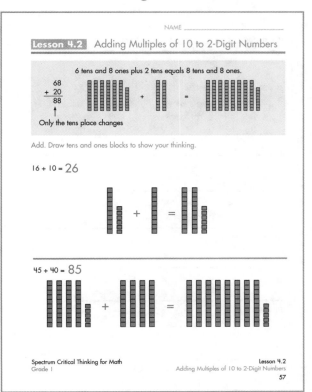

$45 + 40 = 85$

Page 58

NAME _____

Lesson 4.2 Adding Multiples of 10 to 2-Digit Numbers

Add. Draw tens blocks and ones blocks to show your thinking.

$\begin{array}{r} 13 \\ + 30 \\ \hline 43 \end{array}$

$\begin{array}{r} 29 \\ + 50 \\ \hline 79 \end{array}$

$\begin{array}{r} 17 \\ + 60 \\ \hline 77 \end{array}$

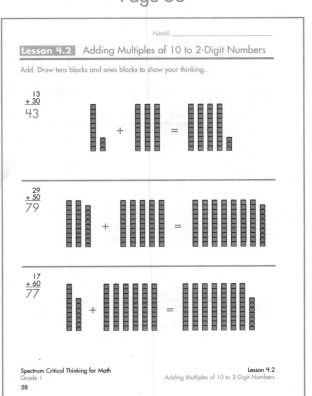

Page 59

NAME _____

Lesson 4.2 Adding Multiples of 10 to 2-Digit Numbers

You can use a number line to add multiples of 10 to 2-digit numbers.

Start at the first 2-digit number you are given. Then, count by how many tens you are adding up the number line. Where you stop is your answer.

$47 + 20 = ?$ 47 57 67 $47 + 20 = 67$

Add. Use a number line to show your thinking.

$42 + 30 = 72$

42   52   62   72

$13 + 80 = 93$

13 23 33 43 53 63 73 83 93

$16 + 20 = 36$

16   26   36

Answer Key

Page 60

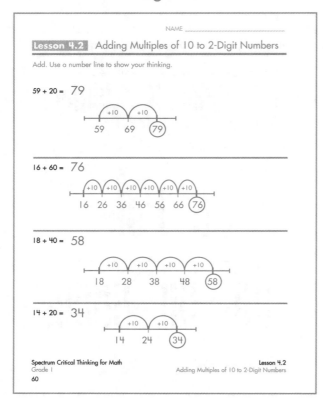

NAME _____

Lesson 4.2 Adding Multiples of 10 to 2-Digit Numbers

Add. Use a number line to show your thinking.

$59 + 20 = 79$

$16 + 60 = 76$

$18 + 40 = 58$

$14 + 20 = 34$

Page 61

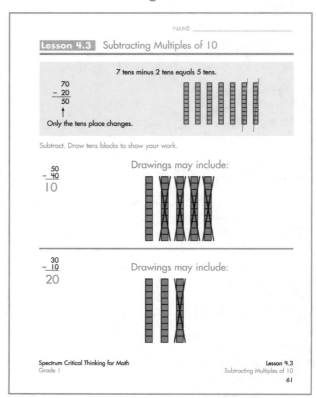

NAME _____

Lesson 4.3 Subtracting Multiples of 10

7 tens minus 2 tens equals 5 tens.

$$\begin{array}{r} 70 \\ -\ 20 \\ \hline 50 \end{array}$$

Only the tens place changes.

Subtract. Draw tens blocks to show your work.

$$\begin{array}{r} 50 \\ -\ 40 \\ \hline 10 \end{array}$$

Drawings may include:

$$\begin{array}{r} 30 \\ -\ 10 \\ \hline 20 \end{array}$$

Drawings may include:

Page 62

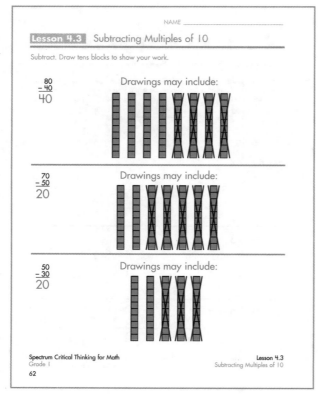

NAME _____

Lesson 4.3 Subtracting Multiples of 10

Subtract. Draw tens blocks to show your work.

$$\begin{array}{r} 80 \\ -\ 40 \\ \hline 40 \end{array}$$

Drawings may include:

$$\begin{array}{r} 70 \\ -\ 50 \\ \hline 20 \end{array}$$

Drawings may include:

$$\begin{array}{r} 50 \\ -\ 30 \\ \hline 20 \end{array}$$

Drawings may include:

Page 63

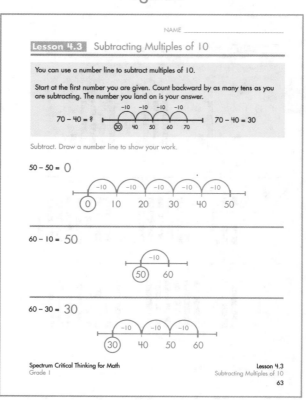

NAME _____

Lesson 4.3 Subtracting Multiples of 10

You can use a number line to subtract multiples of 10.

Start at the first number you are given. Count backward by as many tens as you are subtracting. The number you land on is your answer.

$70 - 40 = ?$ $70 - 40 = 30$

Subtract. Draw a number line to show your work.

$50 - 50 = 0$

$60 - 10 = 50$

$60 - 30 = 30$

Answer Key

Page 64

NAME _____

Lesson 4.4 Adding and Subtracting in the Real World

There are 25 balloons at Austin's birthday party. Austin's mom blows up 30 more balloons. Then, 10 balloons pop. How many balloons are left?

Use tens and ones blocks to show 25 balloons.
Show 30 more balloons.
Cross out the 10 balloons that popped.
Count how many balloons are left.
There are 45 balloons left.

Solve the problem. Use tens and ones blocks to show your thinking.

Bailey needs 10 peaches to make 1 pie. She buys 16 peaches. James brings her 8 more peaches. Does Bailey have enough peaches to make 1 pie?

$16 + 8 =$ ▮▮▮▮▮▮▮▮▮▮ + ▮▮▮▮▮▮▮▮ $= 24$
▮▮▮▮▮▮

Bailey has enough peaches to make a pie because she has more than 10.

Does Bailey have enough peaches to make 2 pies?

She has enough peaches to make 2 pies because she has more than 20.

Page 65

NAME _____

Lesson 4.4 Adding and Subtracting in the Real World

Penny has 18 pencils to start the school year. Vanessa has 9 pencils. A new boy at school forgot his pencils. Penny and Vanessa put their pencils together and gave the boy 6 of them. How many pencils do Penny and Vanessa have left?

Use a number line to show your thinking.

Penny and Vanessa have 21 pencils left.

Solve the problem. Draw a number line to show your thinking.

April rides 24 miles in the car to get to school. Wyatt rides 20 miles. What is the total number of miles that April and Wyatt ride to get to school?

$24 + 20 =$

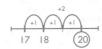

What is the total number of miles they ride to school **and** back home?

April and Wyatt ride 44 total miles to get to school.
$44 + 44 = 88$ total miles to school and back home.

Page 66

NAME _____

Lesson 4.5 Adding 3 Numbers

You can draw a picture with tens and ones blocks to help you add 3 numbers.

```
 12            12
  4             4
+ 3          + 3
            ────
              19
```

Add. Draw tens and ones blocks to show your thinking.

```
 11
  2
+ 6
────
 19
```

```
  5
  4
+ 3
────
 12
```

```
 15
  1
+ 2
────
 18
```

Page 67

NAME _____

Lesson 4.5 Adding 3 Numbers

You can use a number line to help you add 3 numbers. Start your number line at the first number in the problem. Then, count on the amount of the second number. Finally, count on the amount of the last number.
The number you land on is your answer.
$4 + 3 + 2 = ?$
$4 + 3 + 2 = 9$

Add. Use a number line to show your thinking.

$13 + 1 + 3 = 17$

$17 + 1 + 2 = 20$

$3. 5 + 5 + 3 = 13$

117

Answer Key

Page 68

NAME _____

Lesson 4.6 Adding 3 Numbers in the Real World

Blair brought 11 baseballs to baseball practice. Brad brought 3, and Brianna brought 6. After practice, 15 baseballs were left. How many did they lose?

You can write an equation to solve the problem.
11 baseballs + 3 baseballs + 6 baseballs = 20 baseballs
20 baseballs − 15 baseballs = 5 baseballs
They lost 5 baseballs at practice.

Add. Write an equation to show your thinking.

The toy store sold 8 teddy bears in September, 9 in October, and 4 in November. The owner wants to sell 30 teddy bears by the end of December. How many more does the store have to sell to meet that goal?

8 bears + 9 bears + 4 bears = 21 bears
30 bears − 21 bears = 9 bears

The toy store needs to sell 9 more teddy bears to meet its goal.

Craig's Cupcakes sells 3 cupcakes on Sunday, 2 on Monday, and 8 on Tuesday. Last Sunday, Monday and Tuesday, the store sold a total of 15 cupcakes. Did it sell more or fewer cupcakes this week?

3 cupcakes + 2 cupcakes + 8 cupcakes = 13 cupcakes
15 cupcakes is more than 13 cupcakes.

Craig's Cupcakes sold fewer cupcakes this week than last week.

Page 69

NAME _____

Lesson 4.6 Adding 3 Numbers in the Real World

Add. Write an equation to show your thinking.

Caroline ate 5 cherries, 9 grapes, and 1 banana for breakfast. How many pieces of fruit did Caroline eat in all?

$\underline{5} + \underline{9} + \underline{1} = \underline{15}$

Caroline ate $\underline{15}$ pieces of fruit.

Luke ate 2 bites of potatoes, 7 bites of green beans, and 4 bites of baby carrots for dinner. How many bites did Luke eat in all?

$\underline{2} + \underline{7} + \underline{4} = \underline{13}$

Luke ate $\underline{13}$ bites in all.

At the pet store, 5 guinea pigs, 9 fish, and 3 snakes are for sale. How many pets are for sale at the pet store?

$\underline{5} + \underline{9} + \underline{3} = \underline{17}$

$\underline{17}$ pets are for sale at the pet store.

Page 70

NAME _____

💡 **Check What You Learned**

Addition and Subtraction Through 100

Solve the problems. Show your work.

Chase collected 26 ladybugs in one jar. He collected 10 ladybugs in a second jar. He collected 5 ladybugs in a third jar. When he checked the jars the next day, 4 ladybugs had escaped. How many ladybugs were left? Draw tens and ones blocks to show your thinking.

  = 37 ladybugs

Write the equations used to solve the problem.

26 + 10 + 5 = 41
41 − 4 = 37

Addison had 70 nails in her tool belt. She used 20 nails to build a birdhouse. She also used 10 nails to hang the birdhouse in a tree. How many nails are left? Draw a number line to show your thinking.

Write the equation used to solve the problem.

70 − 20 − 10 = 40

CHAPTER 4 POSTTEST

Page 71

NAME _____

🔍 **Check What You Know**

Measurement

1. Kellie drove to work at 7:00 in the morning. Write the time on the clock.

2. Leslie read a book in the park at 11:30 in the morning. Write the time on the clock.

3. Draw one object that is shorter than a spoon. Draw one object that is longer than a spoon.

Drawings will vary, but check to be sure objects drawn would be longer and shorter than a spoon.

CHAPTER 5 PRETEST

Answer Key

Page 72

NAME _____

Check What You Know

Measurement

4. Circle the letter next to the correct way to measure. Write the length of the object.

A.

B.

___8___ dots long

Read the chart. Then, answer the questions.

Allie went to the grocery store. She counted each kind of fruit. Then, she filled out a tally chart showing the amounts of fruit she counted.

🍎	🍌	⚪	🍇
III	HHT II	III	HHT II

4. How many bananas and bunches of grapes did Allie count altogether? __13__

5. Allie counted the same amount for 2 kinds of fruit. Which fruits were they?

___apples___ and ___oranges___

Page 73

NAME _____

Lesson 5.1   Telling and Writing Time to the Hour

Read the story and the questions. Show the answers on the clocks.

Davis and Jayla have a busy day. They get up at 8:00 in the morning. Jayla packs their lunch to eat at the park. Davis gets their flying disc and soccer ball to play with. Davis and Jayla get into the car an hour after they get up. Off to the park they go! They tell Mom they will see her for dinner at 6 in the evening. Davis and Jayla will go to bed 2 hours after dinner.

What time will Davis and Jayla see Mom for dinner?

`6 : 00`

What time do Davis and Jayla get up in the morning?

(clock showing 8:00)

What time do Davis and Jayla get into the car?

`9 : 00`

What time will Davis and Jayla go to bed?

(clock showing 8:00)

Page 74

NAME _____

Lesson 5.2   Telling and Writing Time to the Half Hour

Read the story and the questions. Show the answers on the clocks.

Marisa's class is going on a field trip. The bus leaves at 8:30 in the morning. It will arrive at the aquarium 1 hour later. The class will see the sharks and sting rays first. At 11:30, the class will eat lunch. A half-hour after lunch, they will watch the diving show. At 2:30 in the afternoon, Marisa's class will get on the bus to go home.

What time does Marisa get on the bus to come home?

`2 : 30`

What time does Marisa's class get to the aquarium?

(clock showing 9:30)

What time does Marisa's class watch the diving show?

`12:00`

What time does Marisa's bus leave in the morning?

(clock showing 8:30)

Page 75

NAME _____

Lesson 5.3   Ordering Objects by Size

You can put objects in order by length by comparing two objects to a third object.

The paperclip is shorter than the lollipop. The shovel is longer than the lollipop.

Draw one object that is shorter than the object given. Draw one object that is longer than the object given. Then, fill in the blanks to make each statement true.

Answers will vary. Check for measurement accuracy and correct description of objects.

The _____ is shorter than a pen.

The _____ is longer than a pen.

The _____ is shorter than a pitchfork.

The _____ is longer than a pitchfork.

Answers will vary. Check for measurement accuracy and correct description of objects.

Answer Key

Page 76

Lesson 5.4 Comparing Lengths in the Real World

You can compare lengths of objects by telling what they are longer or shorter than.

The top pencil is longer than the middle pencil and the bottom pencil. The middle pencil is shorter than the top pencil and the bottom pencil. The bottom pencil is shorter than the top pencil, but longer than the middle pencil.

Find and draw 3 objects of different lengths. Then, fill in the blanks to tell which objects are shorter and longer.

Answers will vary.

The _____ is longer than the _____ and

_____.

The _____ is shorter than the _____ and

_____.

The _____ is shorter than the _____, but

longer than the _____.

Page 77

Lesson 5.5 Measuring Length

You can measure the length of objects using smaller unit objects. The unit objects must all be the same size. They must be lined up end to end and touch each other. If the unit objects overlap or do not touch each other, the measurement will be wrong.

The fork is 5 paperclips long.

Circle the letter next to the correct way to measure. Write the length of each object.

A
B

__10__ squares long

A
B

__6__ paperclips long

Page 78

Lesson 5.5 Measuring Length

You can use different unit objects to measure the same length.

Roberto and Rosa measure their pet snake. Roberto says the snake is 9 pens long. Rosa says the snake is 12 crayons long. Which is longer: Roberto's pen or Rosa's crayon?

9 < 12 — It takes fewer pens than crayons to measure the snake. That means Roberto's pen is longer.

Answer the questions. Use <, >, or = to compare the measurements.

First, Maya measures her desk at school with erasers. The desk is 25 erasers long. Then, she measures her desk with building blocks. The desk is 28 building blocks long. Which is longer: an eraser or a building block?

25 < 28 – It takes fewer erasers than building blocks to measure the desk. That means an eraser is longer.

Joey measures the baseball bat with baseballs. The bat is 15 baseballs long. Marco measures the bat with pennies. The bat is 31 pennies long. Which is longer: a baseball or a penny?

15 < 31 – It takes fewer baseballs than pennies to measure the baseball bat. That means a baseball is longer.

Page 79

Lesson 5.6 Collecting Data

Make a food chart for 1 day. Draw a picture to show how many of each type of food you ate.

Fruit   Dairy   Meat/Eggs/Fish
Vegetable   Other Foods

Breakfast	
Lunch	
Dinner	
Snacks	

Use your food chart to answer the questions.

How many of each did you eat?

Fruit _____ Dairy _____

Vegetable _____ Meats/Eggs/Fish _____

Other Foods _____

How many food items did you eat? _____

What food did you eat the most? _____

How much more fruit did you eat than vegetables? _____

Answers will vary but should line up with information gathered on food chart.

Answer Key

Page 80

NAME _____

Lesson 5.6 Collecting Data

Make an insect chart. Ask 10 people to tell you their favorite insect. Use tally marks to show what kind.

			Other	None

Tally Marks
| = 1
|| = 2
||| = 3
|||| = 4
|||| = 5

Use your insect chart to answer the questions.

How many people like 🦋? _____

How many people like 🐞? _____

How many people like 🐜? _____

How many people do not like insects? _____

How may people like an insect that is not on the chart? _____

How many people like 🐞 and 🦋? _____

Answers will vary but should line up with information gathered on insect chart.

Page 81

NAME _____

💡 **Check What You Learned**

Measurement

The movie theater is screening 2 movies at 5:00 in the evening, 8 movies at 6:00, 10 movies at 7:00, and 4 movies at 8:00.

1. Organize the data into a tally chart.

5:00	6:00	7:00	8:00

2. At which time are the most movies screening? Show the answer on both clocks.

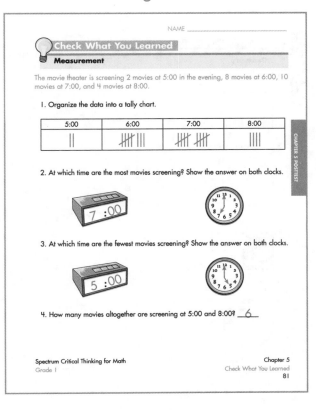

3. At which time are the fewest movies screening? Show the answer on both clocks.

4. How many movies altogether are screening at 5:00 and 8:00? __6__

Page 82

NAME _____

💡 **Check What You Learned**

Measurement

Oliver, Otis, and Obie are measuring their bike ramp. Oliver says the ramp is 7 shoes long. Otis says it is 2 baseball bats long. Obie says it is 9 toy trucks long.

Fill in the blanks to tell which unit objects are shorter and longer.

5. The ___bat___ is longer than the ___shoe___ and ___truck___.

6. The ___truck___ is shorter than the ___shoe___ and ___bat___.

7. The ___shoe___ is shorter than the ___bat___, but longer than the ___truck___.

8. Fill out a chart for the boys' unit objects. Draw pictures to show how many of each object it takes to measure the bike ramp.

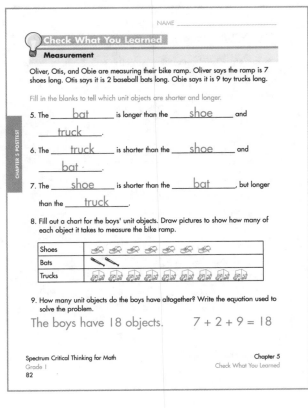

Shoes	👟 👟 👟 👟 👟 👟 👟
Bats	⚾ ⚾
Trucks	🚚 🚚 🚚 🚚 🚚 🚚 🚚 🚚 🚚

9. How many unit objects do the boys have altogether? Write the equation used to solve the problem.

The boys have 18 objects. $7 + 2 + 9 = 18$

Page 83

NAME _____

🔍 **Check What You Know**

Geometry

1. Circle the triangle. Draw a square around the pentagon. Color the rectangle.

2. Draw a real-world example of a circle.

Drawings will vary.

3. Draw a real-world example of a rectangular prism.

Drawings will vary.

Answer Key

Page 84

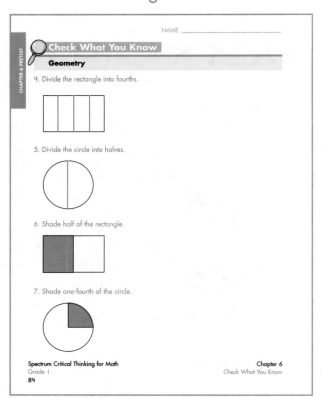

Page 85

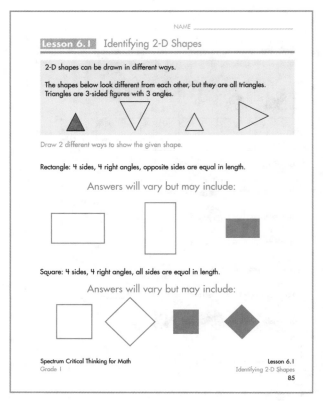

Page 86

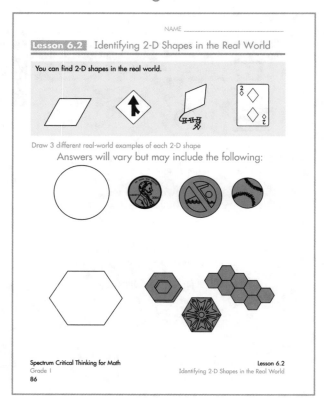

Page 87

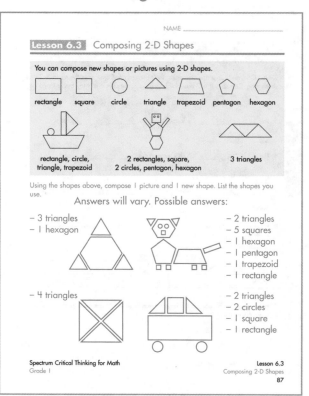

Answer Key

Page 88

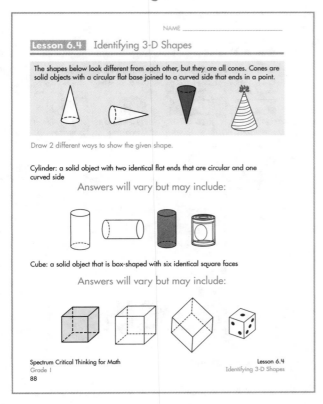

Page 89

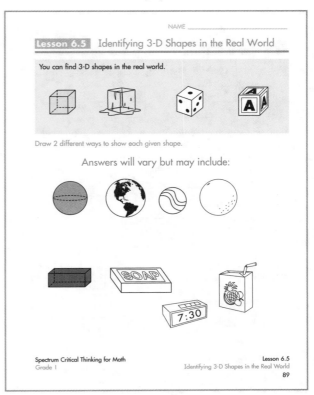

Page 90

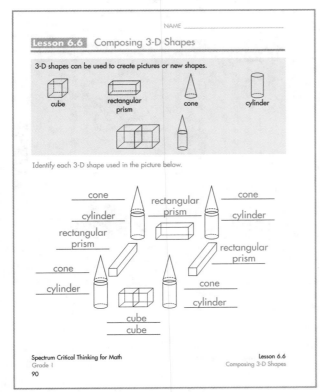

Page 91

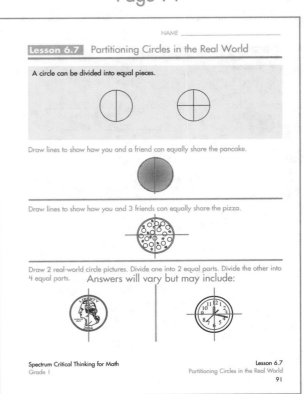

Answer Key

Page 92

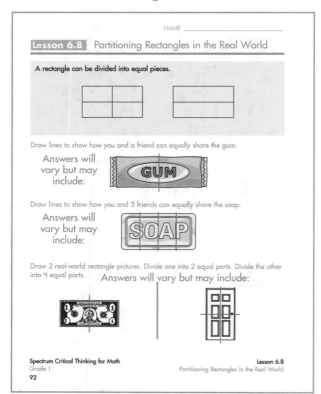

Lesson 6.8 Partitioning Rectangles in the Real World

A rectangle can be divided into equal pieces.

Draw lines to show how you and a friend can equally share the gum.

Answers will vary but may include: GUM

Draw lines to show how you and 3 friends can equally share the soap.

Answers will vary but may include: SOAP

Draw 2 real-world rectangle pictures. Divide one into 2 equal parts. Divide the other into 4 equal parts.

Answers will vary but may include:

Page 93

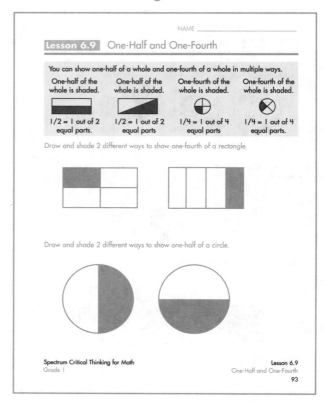

Lesson 6.9 One-Half and One-Fourth

You can show one-half of a whole and one-fourth of a whole in multiple ways.

One-half of the whole is shaded.	One-half of the whole is shaded.	One-fourth of the whole is shaded.	One-fourth of the whole is shaded.
1/2 = 1 out of 2 equal parts.	1/2 = 1 out of 2 equal parts	1/4 = 1 out of 4 equal parts	1/4 = 1 out of 4 equal parts

Draw and shade 2 different ways to show one-fourth of a rectangle.

Draw and shade 2 different ways to show one-half of a circle.

Page 94

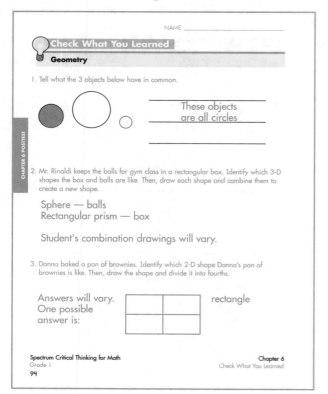

Check What You Learned
Geometry

1. Tell what the 3 objects below have in common.

These objects are all circles

2. Mr. Rinaldi keeps the balls for gym class in a rectangular box. Identify which 3-D shapes the box and balls are like. Then, draw each shape and combine them to create a new shape.

Sphere — balls
Rectangular prism — box

Student's combination drawings will vary.

3. Donna baked a pan of brownies. Identify which 2-D shape Donna's pan of brownies is like. Then, draw the shape and divide it into fourths.

Answers will vary. One possible answer is: rectangle

Page 95

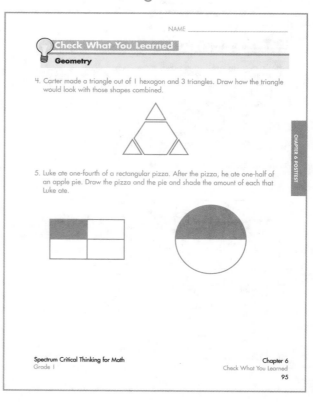

Check What You Learned
Geometry

4. Carter made a triangle out of 1 hexagon and 3 triangles. Draw how the triangle would look with those shapes combined.

5. Luke ate one-fourth of a rectangular pizza. After the pizza, he ate one-half of an apple pie. Draw the pizza and the pie and shade the amount of each that Luke ate.

Answer Key

Page 96

Final Test Chapters 1–6

Solve the problems.

1. Heather and Nadia each had 20 bottles of water to give out at the race. When the race was over, Heather had 5 bottles of water left. Nadia had 6 bottles left. How many bottles of water did both girls give out during the race? Show your answer using tens and ones blocks.

H — 20 – 5 = 15
N — 20 – 6 = 14
H + N gave out 15 + 14 = 29

29 =

2. Forrest collects 55 acorns from the backyard. Anthony collects 30 acorns. How many acorns did they collect altogether? Use a number line to show your answer.

55 + 30

The boys collected 85 acorns altogether.

+10 +10 +10
55   65   75   (85)

3. Forrest and Anthony want to collect 100 acorns altogether. How many more do they need to collect? Write the equation used to solve the problem.

The boys need to collect 15 more acorns.

100 – 85 = 15

Page 97

Final Test Chapters 1–6

Solve the problems.

4. In July, Oliver grew 30 tomatoes in his garden. He gave 20 tomatoes to a neighbor. In August, he grew 40 tomatoes. He gave 30 to a neighbor. How many tomatoes did Oliver keep for himself in July and August? Show your answer using tens blocks.

July — 30 – 20 = = 10

August — 40 – 30 =  = 10

10 + 10 = ▮▮▮▮▮▮▮▮▮▮ = 20

Oliver kept 20 tomatoes for himself in July and August.

5. Did Oliver keep more tomatoes or give away more tomatoes? Compare the numbers. Write <, >, or = in the box.

20 $<$ 50 .

Oliver gave away more tomatoes.

6. Sam's cat had 3 baby kittens. Each kitten weighed 4 pounds. How much did the 3 kittens weigh altogether? Use a number line to show your answer.

4 + 4 + 4 = 12

+1 +1 +1 +1 +1 +1 +1 +1 +1 +1 +1 +1
4   8   (12)

Page 98

Final Test Chapters 1–6

7. Solve. Write the addition problem used.

9 – 3 = __6__   __3__ + __6__ = __9__

8. Use the problem above to fill out the fact family triangle. Write the 4 number sentences in the fact family.

9 – 3 = 6
9 – 6 = 3
3 + 6 = 9
6 + 3 = 9

9. Follow the paths. Count forward or backward to fill in the circles.

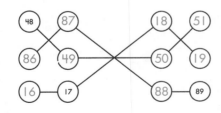

Page 99

Final Test Chapters 1–6

At 3:00 in the afternoon, Rashad started counting his toys. At 3:30, he finished counting and made a chart. Look at his chart. Then, answer the questions.

Trucks	🚂🚂🚂🚂🚂🚂🚂
Stuffed Animals	🧸🐢🦒
Balls	⚽⚽⚽🏀
Robots	🤖🤖🤖🤖

10. How many toys does Rashad have altogether? __18__

11. Does Rashad have more balls or more stuffed animals? Write each number. Then, write <, >, or = in the box.

__4__ $>$ __3__   Rashad has more balls.

12. How many more trucks than robots does Rashad have? Draw a picture to show your thinking.

7 – 4 = 3

13. Write the time Rashad started counting his toys.

14. Write the time Rashad finished counting his toys.

Answer Key

NAME _____

Final Test Chapters 1–6

15. Circle the item that is longer than the crayon. Cross out the item that is shorter than the crayon. Draw an item that is shorter than the toothbrush but longer than the crayon.

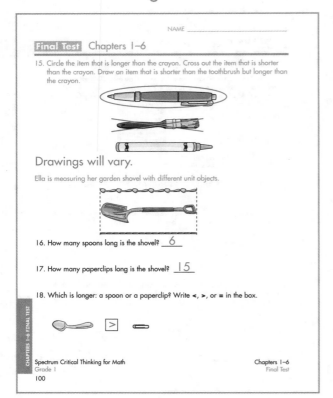

Drawings will vary.

Ella is measuring her garden shovel with different unit objects.

16. How many spoons long is the shovel? __6__

17. How many paperclips long is the shovel? __15__

18. Which is longer: a spoon or a paperclip? Write **<**, **>**, or **=** in the box.

$>$

CHAPTERS 1–6 FINAL TEST

Spectrum Critical Thinking for Math
Grade 1
100

Chapters 1–6
Final Test

NAME _____

Final Test Chapters 1–6

19. Lian cleaned out her backpack. She found a quarter, an envelope, a marble, and a building block. Write the shape name of each object. Draw each shape next to the shape name.

Quarter ___circle___

Envelope ___rectangle___

Marble ___sphere___

Building block ___cube___

20. Yesterday, Cory packed a rectangular candy bar for a snack. He wanted to divide it so he and 3 friends could each have an equal piece. Draw how he divided the candy bar.

Answers will vary but may include:

21. Today, Cory packed a donut. He wanted to divide it so he and 1 other friend could both have an equal piece. Draw how he divided the donut.

Answers will vary but may include:

CHAPTERS 1–6 FINAL TEST

Spectrum Critical Thinking for Math
Grade 1

Chapters 1–6
Final Test
101

Notes

Notes